The Convention on the Elimination of all forms of Discrimination Against Men (CEDAM)

Carl Reinhold Augustsson

Copyright © 2025

Carl Reinhold Augustsson

All Rights Reserved. Any unauthorized reprint or use of this material is strictly prohibited. No part of this book may be reproduced or transmitted in any form or by any means, electronic or mechanical, including photocopying, recording, or by any information storage and retrieval system without express written permission from the author.

All reasonable attempts have been made to verify the accuracy of the information provided in this publication. Nevertheless, the author assumes no responsibility for any errors and/or omissions.

Contents

Dedication 1

Introduction 2

Convention on the Elimination of All Forms of
Discrimination Against Women 16

Convention on the Elimination of All Forms of
Discrimination Against Men 39

My Modest Proposal 62

Chennai Train Rides and Their Implications 64

An Open Letter to Feminism 67

An Open Letter to Women 69

Georgian Funerals 71

Making the Republic of Georgia Ideal for Everyone 78

Military Conscription: Perhaps the biggest example of
sexism in Western Civilization today 83

Sexköpslagen 111

On the Notion that Legal Sex Work Leads to Trafficking
.... 117

The Supplemental DS-157 Nonimmigrant Visa Application
Form 123

The "Hawk Tuah" Girl 129

The Conservative Case in Favor of San Francisco's
Proposed Ban on Male Circumcision 131

Special Occasions 143

The Crux of the Issue 149

How Men's Rights Has Made Me Anti-War 155

In Defense of "Incels" 162

Bavarian Business Attire 167

I Used to Adore Feminism 171

Final Thoughts 173

Dedication

To all the young men, worldwide, throughout the ages, who have died as unwilling conscripts in wars that they often didn't agree with or even fully understand, who, if they had merely been born female, would have not been forced to fight in the first place.

Introduction

In the 1970s, the United Nations passed the Convention on the Elimination of all Forms of Discrimination Against Women (CEDAW). It has been ratified by nearly all of the world's independent states. While CEDAW represents a great step forward in the name of gender equality, it—as the name itself would imply—is only half of the story. The time has, therefore, long come for a male equivalent: a Convention on the Elimination of all Forms of Discrimination Against Men (CEDAM).

I have therefore, on my own initiative, decided to create a Convention on the Elimination of all Forms of Discrimination Against Men, to be modeled on the equivalent for women. What follows is a copy of my initiative.

There are a couple of points that I wish to emphasize from the outset. First of all, I am by no means trying to diminish the Convention on the Elimination of all Forms of Discrimination Against Women. On the contrary, the first clause of the preamble reaffirms the goals set out in CEDAW: "Reaffirming the goals set out in the Convention on the Elimination of All Forms of Discrimination Against Women." Indeed, many of the points mentioned in CEDAW, if fully implemented, would benefit men as well. Case in point, article 11 (especially section e) states:

> States Parties shall take all appropriate measures to eliminate discrimination against women in the field of employment in order to ensure, on a basis of equality of men and women, the same rights, in particular:
>
> (e) The right to social security, particularly in cases of retirement, unemployment, sickness, invalidity and old age and other incapacity to work, as well as the right to paid leave;

What is noteworthy about this is that it calls for men and women to have equal access to retirement. If only this were the case. Up until recently, the majority of European states (among others) had higher retirement age for men than for women. Any moves towards equal access—which is thankfully occurring more and more—would actually benefit men since it is men and not women who face discrimination in this area. However, if the unofficial definition of equality is "the absence of discrimination against women"—which it should never be! —then, I suppose that higher retirement ages for men would not violate this clause of CEDAW. I have reiterated this point in CEDAM in article 13:

> States Parties shall take all appropriate measures to ensure that all age requirements, in both the public and private spheres, apply equally to men as well as women, including but not limited to:
>
> > (a) Retirement age;

(b) Minimum age for withdrawing from pension funds;

(c) Minimum age for collecting state benefits for the elderly;

(d) Minimum age for marriage;

(e) Minimum age for early release from prison for older people;

(f) Minimum age for the buying, possession, and consumption of controlled substances such as alcohol;

(g) Minimum age for entrance into business establishments.

Also, CEDAW unfortunately made no reference to female genital mutilation. CEDAM, however, mentions the genital integrity for both boys and girls.

It is for this reason that I am including a copy of CEDAW *before* introducing my CEDAM initiative. Indeed, there simply is no better way to introduce a proposed CEDAM treaty than by first mentioning CEDAW.

The other point I wish to establish is that this initiative is not merely for want of having a male equivalent to CEDAW "just to have one." Instead, there is a real need for a Convention on the Elimination of all Forms of Discrimination Against Men. It is at this point that I wish to emphasize that there are no pure hypotheticals listed in

CEDAM, i.e., I did not just "sit around" and dream up areas in which sexism against men could *possibly* exist. Most of the 46 articles listed here mention an actual, present-day example of discrimination or violence uniquely or disproportionally faced by men and boys somewhere in the world. In some cases, the articles mention examples of sexism against men, which have at least historically existed. Likewise, a few of the points raised are based on sexist proposals that have been suggested, even if, thankfully, have never actually been implemented. Finally, in a handful of cases, some points were included in an article so as to ensure that "all bases were touched."

If several of these points were the only examples of discrimination or violence against men or boys in the world today, then perhaps a CEDAM would not be necessary. After all, it would probably be enough to simply fight against those few examples on their own.

However, there is an even greater need for a CEDAM than the 46 individual points raised in it. That need is addressed in the fourteen clauses of the preamble. First and foremost, the basis upon which the equality debate rests seems to be that only women faced discrimination, whereas men were privileged. The truth is that both men and women were forced into gender roles, like it or not. In essence, there were two gender "packages"; the package that each individual "received" was determined at birth. Each package came with its own share of advantages and disadvantages.

As to which package was the better of the two largely depended on one's personal preferences. For example, for a man who had no interest in politics, didn't want to do military service (in the times and places when it was required), and would have rather stayed home with the children than go out and have a career, being a man really would not have seemed like much of a privilege. By contrast, for a woman who also had no interest in politics, was glad that she did not have to do military service, and enjoyed staying home with the children with no interest in a career, being a woman, if anything, would have seemed like a privilege, especially when one considers the chivalrous ways in which men (at least in Western countries) were supposed to treat women. There is no doubt that such men and women have existed throughout history. It is, therefore, highly oversimplified at best to claim that men were privileged.

Instead, as I have just stated, the reality was that both sexes have had their share of privileges and discrimination. This means that there never was a "patriarchy," and if there ever was one, there certainly isn't one now. Moreover, if there ever was a patriarchy, a huge part of it was the belief that women's lives are more valuable than men's. Instead, the reality was that both sexes faced discrimination, just in different ways. If I accomplish nothing else with this CEDAM initiative, I hope to at least finally establish this as society's view of the history of gender roles, instead of the current one-sided view. Indeed, if society would just finally realize that truth, most, if not all, of the 46 articles in CEDAM would immediately or at least shortly be accomplished.

At this point, I will explain the rest of the points in the CEDAM initiative. However, I do not intend to explain them all, as I want CEDAM to largely speak for itself. First of all, I want to explain the preamble. As I have already mentioned, the most important part of the preamble is establishing the fact that there never was a patriarchy; instead, both men and women faced discrimination, only in different ways, and that discrimination against men both exists and is just as wrong as discrimination against women. After all, the first point made in the preamble is to reaffirm the goals set out in the Convention on the Elimination of all forms of Discrimination Against Women. Again, it needs to be emphasized that CEDAM is not designed to counter CEDAW. Instead, it is designed to complement it. Furthermore, while feminism may be to blame for some of these points, it is not to be blamed for all of them.

Another important point I wanted to make in the preamble is that most men are honorable, decent citizens and are not rapists, pedophiles, or abusive in general. Sadly, there has been so much male bashing that these seemingly obvious points need to be made. Likewise, there is a clause emphasizing the importance of healthy human sexuality that has also been sadly bashed by feminists as well. The other points raised in the preamble include the fact that societies need both men and women and that there will never be sexual equality in general without equality for men as well.

The body of CEDAM comprises 46 articles. First of all, I wish to again state that none of these 46 points are purely hypotheticals. These 46 articles are grouped into 5 different parts. Generally speaking, the more important parts are listed first. That does not mean, however, that the articles towards the end are of little importance.

The first part deals with matters of life and death, and health. The exception to that is the first article, which is about International Men's Day. While the establishment of International Men's Day is hardly the most important article in CEDAM, it is a logical place to start. CEDAM only calls for the adoption of International Men's Day in the states that recognize International Women's Day. After all, the point is equality and balance. Furthermore, article 1 makes it clear that a Veterans' Day, though laudable, is not the same as a Men's Day. The reason that it was included is because in the former Soviet Union and in some of its former republics, like Russia, there was/is a Veterans' Day, which is seen as an unofficial Men's Day. Indeed, it is often referred to as "Men's Day." While a day for veterans is great, it should not be seen as a Men's Day since it is based on conscription, which is truly one of the greatest examples of a sexist injustice.

The rest of part I deals with issues of life and death, bodily integrity, and health. Generally speaking, men—far from being privileged—have been seen as being the "disposable sex." Two major examples of this include conscription and the idea that women should be evacuated from dangerous situations before men, assuming men are even evacuated at all.

Another major issue in part I is that of genital integrity. Many feminists cannot stand seeing male circumcision compared to female genital mutilation. It is important to remember several facts regarding this. First of all, lumping two or more things into the same category does not imply that they are at the same level. After all, calling both armed robbery and murder "felonies" should not be seen as an insult to the victims of murder just because the two are in the same category, even though murder is clearly worse than armed robbery.

Likewise, there are a number of different types of female genital mutilation, as not all involve stitching the labia together. Some variants involve removing all or even just some of the clitoral hood. It is hard to argue that that is at the same level as male circumcision, let alone worse. However, opponents of female genital mutilation rightly condemn all forms, even a substitute pinprick of the labia. They see no need to excuse the lesser forms for the want of condemning the more severe forms. The law in the US and other countries against female genital mutilation bans all forms. In short, all children, both male and female, are entitled to intact genitals, and therefore, all forms of genital cutting of minors should be lumped into the same category as "genital mutilation" and should be illegal. It is sexist *not* to compare male circumcision to female genital mutilation.

Also included in part I is an article against all other forms of "painful rite of passage ceremonies, especially those involving the cutting of the body." In addition, part I also includes articles about men's health, and an article about the blood feuds of northern Albania.

The second part is about legal requirements for men, beyond those involving military service. The biggest example of this is higher tax rates for men, which fortunately does not occur in many states but is found in some.

The most common examples of separate legal requirements for men (outside of military-related issues) are higher minimum age for men. The most common higher minimum age for men are with regards to retirement age and minimum age for marriage.

Also mentioned in part II are the restrictions that the city of Chennai, India, made on men on commuter trains after the lifting of pandemic restrictions (see my article on this in the second half of this book). Also from India, there was a proposal in New Delhi (I am not sure whether it was ever implemented) that in order to ease traffic congestion, drivers would be restricted to only driving on certain days, based on their license plates. However, women drivers would be exempt from this restriction. This clearly constitutes sexism against men.

Article 17 references civil obligations. I remember, following the death of Supreme Court Justice Ruth Bader Ginsburg, reading an article about all the amazing things she had done as a lawyer. In one case, there was a US state that had a jury duty obligation for men only. She successfully represented a man who felt that that was sexist. Also, I wanted to cover any other non-military service legal obligations that apply only or even mainly to men.

Under article 18, the separate and completely useless additional visa application form which the United States began to require of men between the ages of 16 and 45 following the attacks of September 11 (Side note, the United States now uses an online visa application that runs a number of web pages long. I am therefore not sure whether men are still sexistly required to provide additional information for a United States visa. See my article about this visa form in the articles section of this book.).

The last article of Part II mentions obligations to elderly parents. I remember reading an article over a decade ago that stated that part of the reason so many Chinese parents wanted a son (back when China had its one child policy) was because under Chinese law, adult sons are legally obliged to look after their parents in old age, whereas adult daughters have no such obligation.

The third part is about crime and safety, along with the issue of hate speech laws. There are articles discussing perversions to the criminal justice system that have occurred as a result of radical feminism. Such examples include false accusations of rape, pedophilia, and domestic violence, along with ignoring male victims of domestic violence, sexual assault and treating all men as potential rapists and pedophiles. Likewise, part III also addresses some of the abuses of things such as sex offender registries and the prosecution of minors for sexual acts between each other. In addition, part III also deals with the harsher way in which the criminal justice system treats men. Finally, part III addresses safety policies that are tantamount to discrimination against men. Such examples include women-only compartments in trains and subways, women-only establishments (like taxis and hotels), taxis offering women discounts at night, and only allowing women to carry certain weapons.

Part IV deals with dating, marriage, fatherhood, and sexuality. In this part, the importance of marriage and fatherhood are addressed, along with the plight of divorced men and non-custodial fathers, as well as issues such as paternity fraud. In addition, this part covers the attacks on sexuality, including feminist attacks on things such as pornography, strip clubs, and prostitution. Also mentioned are society's sexist expectations placed on men with regard to the dating process and unreasonable policies with regard to sexual harassment and consent.

Part V is about education, employment, and business practices. It discusses issues such as affirmative action, boys falling behind girls in school, and businesses either banning men or charging men more (whatever justification these businesses use for such practices). Part V also mentions special occasions and clothing issues (see my articles about these topics in the second half of this book).

This CEDAM proposal was designed to cover nearly all forms of discrimination and/or violence against men and boys, no matter where in the world they occur. However, this list is not necessarily completely exhausted, as there may be other examples of sexism against males that I am unaware of.

At the same time, while CEDAM was designed to cover all examples of discrimination against males, it purposely avoids getting involved in unrelated issues. There are two issues that were specifically avoided at all costs: abortion and homosexuality. I strongly ask that any CEDAM treaty avoid these two issues.

Moreover, CEDAW established a committee to oversee its implementation. Perhaps a similar committee should be established for the implementation of CEDAM. Indeed, CEDAW led to a UNWOMEN. It is time for the creation of a UNMEN.

It is also important to note that this is obviously just a rough draft. After all, if and when a member state of the United Nations agrees to sponsor this, there is a strong chance that this will be revised. Likewise, perhaps there are things that should be added to it.

Right now, I am attempting to find a member state of the United Nations to introduce CEDAM. I have written separate letters to all 193 member states of the United Nations. Whenever possible, I wrote in the language of the member state in question. I have not received many responses, but I will continue to press for a sponsor. I am willing to visit any of these 193 states in order to present this plan. Furthermore, I am willing to work with absolutely anyone who is willing to work with me.

The second half of this book includes a number of articles that I have written about these issues during the decade and a half that I have been active in the men's rights movement. They appear in no particular order, although the last six, starting with "Special Occasions," are new articles that have never appeared anywhere else before.

I have sadly experienced a number of people hostile to men's rights over the years, even though nothing listed here is extreme or anti-women. I urge all of you to read this without being defensive and realizing that you don't have to disagree with the points made here.

There are several thoughts with which I want to leave you:

> "The biggest example of sexism in the world today is the ridiculous notion that only one sex has ever been the victim of it";

> "The unofficial definition of gender equality must never be allowed to be 'the absence of discrimination against women'";

"With nastiness towards none, genital integrity for all, and military service obligations for none, I am a men's rights advocate."

Please watch the video explanation on YouTube (This video is fairly old, and is therefore based on an older draft of this initiative:

https://www.youtube.com/watch?v=ExqguEBTqtk&fbclid=IwAR1N8c_3zl45Nj08d5oeEfTUWBnzZHnjnSkjqc8FVt6Ulbn7dPgox_johO4

And Please visit the Facebook Page: The Convention on the Elimination of all Forms of Discrimination Against Men (CEDAM)

Convention on the Elimination of All Forms of Discrimination Against Women

The States Parties to the present Convention,

-Noting that the Charter of the United Nations reaffirms faith in fundamental human rights, in the dignity and worth of the human person, and in the equal rights of men and women,

Noting that the Universal Declaration of Human Rights affirms the principle of the inadmissibility of discrimination and proclaims that all human beings are born free and equal in dignity and rights and that everyone is entitled to all the rights and freedoms set forth therein, without distinction of any kind, including distinction based on sex,

Noting that the States Parties to the International Covenants on Human Rights have the obligation to ensure the equal rights of men and women to enjoy all economic, social, cultural, civil and political rights,

Considering the international conventions concluded under the auspices of the United Nations and the specialized agencies promoting the equality of rights of men and women,

Noting also the resolutions, declarations, and recommendations adopted by the United Nations and the specialized agencies promoting the equality of rights of men and women,

Concerned, however, that despite these various instruments, extensive discrimination against women continues to exist,

Recalling that discrimination against women violates the principles of equality of rights and respect for human dignity, is an obstacle to the participation of women on equal terms with men in the political, social, economic, and cultural life of their countries, hampers the growth of the prosperity of society and the family and makes more difficult the full development of the potentialities of women in the service of their countries and of humanity,

Concerned that in situations of poverty, women have the least access to food, health, education, training, and opportunities for employment and other needs,

Convinced that the establishment of the new international economic order based on equity and justice will contribute significantly towards the promotion of equality between men and women,

Emphasizing that the eradication of apartheid, all forms of racism, racial discrimination, colonialism, neo-colonialism, aggression, foreign occupation, and domination and interference in the internal affairs of States is essential to the full enjoyment of the rights of men and women,

Affirming that the strengthening of international peace and security, the relaxation of international tension, mutual cooperation among all States irrespective of their social and economic systems, general and complete disarmament, in particular nuclear disarmament under strict and effective international control, the affirmation of the principles of justice, equality and mutual benefit in relations among countries and the realization of the right of peoples under alien and colonial domination and foreign occupation to self-determination and independence, as well as respect for national sovereignty and territorial integrity, will promote social progress and development and as a consequence will contribute to the attainment of full equality between men and women,

Convinced that the full and complete development of a country, the welfare of the world, and the cause of peace require the maximum participation of women on equal terms with men in all fields,

Bearing in mind the great contribution of women to the welfare of the family and to the development of society, so far not fully recognized, the social significance of maternity and the role of both parents in the family and in the upbringing of children and aware that the role of women in procreation should not be a basis for discrimination but that the upbringing of children requires a sharing of responsibility between men and women and society as a whole,

Aware that a change in the traditional role of men as well as the role of women in society and in the family is needed to achieve full equality between men and women,

Determined to implement the principles set forth in the Declaration on the Elimination of Discrimination against

Women and, for that purpose, to adopt the measures required for the elimination of such discrimination in all its forms and manifestations,

Have agreed on the following:

PART I

Article 1

-For the purposes of the present Convention, the term "discrimination against women" shall mean any distinction, exclusion or restriction made on the basis of sex which has the effect or purpose of impairing or nullifying the recognition, enjoyment or exercise by women, irrespective of their marital status, on a basis of equality of men and women, of human rights and fundamental freedoms in the political, economic, social, cultural, civil or any other field.

Article 2

-States Parties condemn discrimination against women in all its forms, agree to pursue by all appropriate means and without delay a policy of eliminating discrimination against women and, to this end, undertake:

- -(a) To embody the principle of the equality of men and women in their national constitutions or other appropriate legislation if not yet incorporated therein and to ensure, through law and other appropriate means, the practical realization of this principle;

(b) To adopt appropriate legislative and other measures, including sanctions where appropriate, prohibiting all discrimination against women;

(c) To establish legal protection of the rights of women on an equal basis with men and to ensure through competent national tribunals and other public institutions the effective protection of women against any act of discrimination;

(d) To refrain from engaging in any act or practice of discrimination against women and to ensure that public authorities and institutions shall act in conformity with this obligation;

(e) To take all appropriate measures to eliminate discrimination against women by any person, organization or enterprise;

(f) To take all appropriate measures, including legislation, to modify or abolish existing laws, regulations, customs and practices which constitute discrimination against women;

(g) To repeal all national penal provisions which constitute discrimination against women.

Article 3

-States Parties shall take in all fields, in particular in the political, social, economic and cultural fields, all appropriate measures, including legislation, to ensure the full development and advancement of women , for the purpose of guaranteeing them the exercise and enjoyment of human rights and fundamental freedoms on a basis of equality with men.

Article 4

-1. Adoption by States Parties of temporary special measures aimed at accelerating de facto equality between men and women shall not be considered discrimination as defined in the present Convention, but shall in no way entail as a consequence the maintenance of unequal or separate standards; these measures shall be discontinued when the objectives of equality of opportunity and treatment have been achieved.

2. Adoption by States Parties of special measures, including those measures contained in the present Convention, aimed at protecting maternity shall not be considered discriminatory.

Article 5

-States Parties shall take all appropriate measures:

- -(a) To modify the social and cultural patterns of conduct of men and women, with a view to achieving the elimination of prejudices and customary and all other practices which are based on the idea of the inferiority or the superiority of either of the sexes or on stereotyped roles for men and women;

(b) To ensure that family education includes a proper understanding of maternity as a social function and the recognition of the common responsibility of men and women in the upbringing and development of their children, it being understood that the interest of the children is the primordial consideration in all cases.

Article 6

-States Parties shall take all appropriate measures, including legislation, to suppress all forms of traffic in women and exploitation of prostitution of women.

PART II

Article 7

-States Parties shall take all appropriate measures to eliminate discrimination against women in the political and public life of the country and, in particular, shall ensure to women, on equal terms with men, the right:

- -(a) To vote in all elections and public referenda and to be eligible for election to all publicly elected bodies;

(b) To participate in the formulation of government policy and the implementation thereof and to hold public office and perform all public functions at all levels of government;

(c) To participate in non-governmental organizations and associations concerned with the public and political life of the country.

Article 8

-States Parties shall take all appropriate measures to ensure to women, on equal terms with men and without any discrimination, the opportunity to represent their

Governments at the international level and to participate in the work of international organizations.

Article 9

-1. States Parties shall grant women equal rights with men to acquire, change or retain their nationality. They shall ensure in particular that neither marriage to an alien nor change of nationality by the husband during marriage shall automatically change the nationality of the wife, render her stateless or force upon her the nationality of the husband.

2. States Parties shall grant women equal rights with men with respect to the nationality of their children.

PART III

Article 10

-States Parties shall take all appropriate measures to eliminate discrimination against women in order to ensure to them equal rights with men in the field of education and in particular to ensure, on a basis of equality of men and women:

- -(a) The same conditions for career and vocational guidance, for access to studies and for the achievement of diplomas in educational establishments of all categories in rural as well as in urban areas; this equality shall be ensured in pre-school, general, technical, professional and higher technical education, as well as in all types of vocational training;

(b) Access to the same curricula, the same examinations, teaching staff with qualifications of the same standard and school premises and equipment of the same quality;

(c) The elimination of any stereotyped concept of the roles of men and women at all levels and in all forms of education by encouraging coeducation and other types of education which will help to achieve this aim and, in particular, by the revision of textbooks and school programmes and the adaptation of teaching methods;

(d) The same opportunities to benefit from scholarships and other study grants;

(e) The same opportunities for access to programmes of continuing education, including adult and functional literacy programmes, particulary those aimed at reducing, at the earliest possible time, any gap in education existing between men and women;

(f) The reduction of female student drop-out rates and the organization of programmes for girls and women who have left school prematurely;

(g) The same Opportunities to participate actively in sports and physical education;

(h) Access to specific educational information to help to ensure the health and well-being of families, including information and advice on family planning.

Article 11

-1. States Parties shall take all appropriate measures to eliminate discrimination against women in the field of employment in order to ensure, on a basis of equality of men and women, the same rights, in particular:

- -(a) The right to work as an inalienable right of all human beings;

(b) The right to the same employment opportunities, including the application of the same criteria for selection in matters of employment;

(c) The right to free choice of profession and employment, the right to promotion, job security and all benefits and conditions of service and the right to receive vocational training and retraining, including apprenticeships, advanced vocational training and recurrent training;

(d) The right to equal remuneration, including benefits, and to equal treatment in respect of work of equal value, as well as equality of treatment in the evaluation of the quality of work;

(e) The right to social security, particularly in cases of retirement, unemployment, sickness, invalidity and old age and other incapacity to work, as well as the right to paid leave;

(f) The right to protection of health and to safety in working conditions, including the safeguarding of the function of reproduction.

-2. In order to prevent discrimination against women on the grounds of marriage or maternity and to ensure their effective right to work, States Parties shall take appropriate measures:

- -(a) To prohibit, subject to the imposition of sanctions, dismissal on the grounds of pregnancy or of maternity leave and discrimination in dismissals on the basis of marital status;

(b) To introduce maternity leave with pay or with comparable social benefits without loss of former employment, seniority or social allowances;

(c) To encourage the provision of the necessary supporting social services to enable parents to combine family obligations with work responsibilities and participation in public life, in particular through promoting the establishment and development of a network of child-care facilities;

(d) To provide special protection to women during pregnancy in types of work proved to be harmful to them.

-3. Protective legislation relating to matters covered in this article shall be reviewed periodically in the light of scientific and technological knowledge and shall be revised, repealed or extended as necessary.

Article 12

-1. States Parties shall take all appropriate measures to eliminate discrimination against women in the field of health care in order to ensure, on a basis of equality of men and women, access to health care services, including those related to family planning.

2. Notwithstanding the provisions of paragraph I of this article, States Parties shall ensure to women appropriate services in connection with pregnancy, confinement and the post-natal period, granting free services where necessary, as well as adequate nutrition during pregnancy and lactation.

Article 13

-States Parties shall take all appropriate measures to eliminate discrimination against women in other areas of economic and social life in order to ensure, on a basis of equality of men and women, the same rights, in particular:

- -(a) The right to family benefits;

(b) The right to bank loans, mortgages and other forms of financial credit;

(c) The right to participate in recreational activities, sports and all aspects of cultural life.

Article 14

-1. States Parties shall take into account the particular problems faced by rural women and the significant roles which rural women play in the economic survival of their families, including their work in the non-monetized sectors of the economy, and shall take all appropriate measures to ensure the application of the provisions of the present Convention to women in rural areas.

2. States Parties shall take all appropriate measures to eliminate discrimination against women in rural areas in order to ensure, on a basis of equality of men and women, that they participate in and benefit from rural development and, in particular, shall ensure to such women the right:

- -(a) To participate in the elaboration and implementation of development planning at all levels;

(b) To have access to adequate health care facilities, including information, counselling and services in family planning;

(c) To benefit directly from social security programmes;

(d) To obtain all types of training and education, formal and non-formal, including that relating to functional literacy, as well as, inter alia, the benefit of all community and extension services, in order to increase their technical proficiency;

(e) To organize self-help groups and co-operatives in order to obtain equal access to economic opportunities through employment or self employment;

(f) To participate in all community activities;

(g) To have access to agricultural credit and loans, marketing facilities, appropriate technology and equal treatment in land and agrarian reform as well as in land resettlement schemes;

(h) To enjoy adequate living conditions, particularly in relation to housing, sanitation, electricity and water supply, transport and communications.

PART IV

Article 15

-1. States Parties shall accord to women equality with men before the law.

2. States Parties shall accord to women, in civil matters, a legal capacity identical to that of men and the same opportunities to exercise that capacity. In particular, they shall give women equal rights to conclude contracts and to administer property and shall treat them equally in all stages of procedure in courts and tribunals.

3. States Parties agree that all contracts and all other private instruments of any kind with a legal effect which is directed at restricting the legal capacity of women shall be deemed null and void.

4. States Parties shall accord to men and women the same rights with regard to the law relating to the movement of persons and the freedom to choose their residence and domicile.

Article 16

-1. States Parties shall take all appropriate measures to eliminate discrimination against women in all matters relating to marriage and family relations and in particular shall ensure, on a basis of equality of men and women:

- -(a) The same right to enter into marriage;

(b) The same right freely to choose a spouse and to enter into marriage only with their free and full consent;

(c) The same rights and responsibilities during marriage and at its dissolution;

(d) The same rights and responsibilities as parents, irrespective of their marital status, in matters relating to their children; in all cases the interests of the children shall be paramount;

(e) The same rights to decide freely and responsibly on the number and spacing of their children and to have access to the information, education and means to enable them to exercise these rights;

(f) The same rights and responsibilities with regard to guardianship, wardship, trusteeship and adoption of children, or similar institutions where these concepts exist in national legislation; in all cases the interests of the children shall be paramount;

(g) The same personal rights as husband and wife, including the right to choose a family name, a profession and an occupation;

(h) The same rights for both spouses in respect of the ownership, acquisition, management, administration, enjoyment and disposition of property, whether free of charge or for a valuable consideration.

-2. The betrothal and the marriage of a child shall have no legal effect, and all necessary action, including legislation, shall be taken to specify a minimum age for marriage and to make the registration of marriages in an official registry compulsory.

PART V

Article 17

-1. For the purpose of considering the progress made in the implementation of the present Convention, there shall be established a Committee on the Elimination of Discrimination against Women (hereinafter referred to as the Committee) consisting, at the time of entry into force of the Convention, of eighteen and, after ratification of or accession to the Convention by the thirty-fifth State Party, of twenty-three experts of high moral standing and competence in the field covered by the Convention. The experts shall be elected by States Parties from among their nationals and shall serve in their personal capacity, consideration being given to equitable geographical distribution and to the representation of the different forms of civilization as well as the principal legal systems.

2. The members of the Committee shall be elected by secret ballot from a list of persons nominated by States Parties. Each State Party may nominate one person from among its own nationals.

3. The initial election shall be held six months after the date of the entry into force of the present Convention. At least three months before the date of each election the Secretary-General of the United Nations shall address a letter to the States Parties inviting them to submit their nominations within two months. The Secretary-General shall prepare a list in alphabetical order of all persons thus nominated, indicating the States Parties which have nominated them, and shall submit it to the States Parties.

4. Elections of the members of the Committee shall be held at a meeting of States Parties convened by the Secretary-General at United Nations Headquarters. At that meeting, for which two thirds of the States Parties shall constitute a quorum, the persons elected to the Committee shall be those nominees who obtain the largest number of votes and an absolute majority of the votes of the representatives of States Parties present and voting.

5. The members of the Committee shall be elected for a term of four years. However, the terms of nine of the members elected at the first election shall expire at the end of two years; immediately after the first election the names of these nine members shall be chosen by lot by the Chairman of the Committee.

6. The election of the five additional members of the Committee shall be held in accordance with the provisions of paragraphs 2, 3 and 4 of this article, following the thirty-fifth ratification or accession. The terms of two of the additional members elected on this occasion shall expire at

the end of two years, the names of these two members having been chosen by lot by the Chairman of the Committee.

7. For the filling of casual vacancies, the State Party whose expert has ceased to function as a member of the Committee shall appoint another expert from among its nationals, subject to the approval of the Committee.

8. The members of the Committee shall, with the approval of the General Assembly, receive emoluments from United Nations resources on such terms and conditions as the Assembly may decide, having regard to the importance of the Committee's responsibilities.

9. The Secretary-General of the United Nations shall provide the necessary staff and facilities for the effective performance of the functions of the Committee under the present Convention.

Article 18

-1. States Parties undertake to submit to the Secretary-General of the United Nations, for consideration by the Committee, a report on the legislative, judicial, administrative or other measures which they have adopted to give effect to the provisions of the present Convention and on the progress made in this respect:

- -(a) Within one year after the entry into force for the State concerned;

(b) Thereafter at least every four years and further whenever the Committee so requests.

-2. Reports may indicate factors and difficulties affecting the degree of fulfilment of obligations under the present Convention.

Article 19

-1. The Committee shall adopt its own rules of procedure.

2. The Committee shall elect its officers for a term of two years.

Article 20

-1. The Committee shall normally meet for a period of not more than two weeks annually in order to consider the reports submitted in accordance with article 18 of the present Convention.

2. The meetings of the Committee shall normally be held at United Nations Headquarters or at any other convenient place as determined by the Committee.

Article 21

-1. The Committee shall, through the Economic and Social Council, report annually to the General Assembly of the United Nations on its activities and may make suggestions and general recommendations based on the examination of report and information received from the States Parties. Such suggestions and general recommendations shall be included in the report of the Committee together with comments, if any, from States Parties.

2. The Secretary-General of the United Nations shall transmit the reports of the Committee to the Commission on the Status of Women for its information.

Article 22

-The specialized agencies shall be entitled to be represented at the consideration of the implementation of such provisions of the present Convention as fall within the scope of their activities. The Committee may invite the specialized agencies to submit reports on the implementation of the Convention in areas falling within the scope of their activities.

PART VI

Article 23

-Nothing in the present Convention shall affect any provisions that are more conducive to the achievement of equality between men and women which may be contained:

- -(a) In the legislation of a State Party; or

(b) In any other international convention, treaty or agreement in force for that State.

Article 24

-States Parties undertake to adopt all necessary measures at the national level aimed at achieving the full realization of the rights recognized in the present Convention.

Article 25

-1. The present Convention shall be open for signature by all States.

2. The Secretary-General of the United Nations is designated as the depositary of the present Convention.

3. The present Convention is subject to ratification. Instruments of ratification shall be deposited with the Secretary-General of the United Nations.

4. The present Convention shall be open to accession by all States. Accession shall be effected by the deposit of an instrument of accession with the Secretary-General of the United Nations.

Article 26

-1. A request for the revision of the present Convention may be made at any time by any State Party by means of a notification in writing addressed to the Secretary-General of the United Nations.

2. The General Assembly of the United Nations shall decide upon the steps, if any, to be taken in respect of such a request.

Article 27

-1. The present Convention shall enter into force on the thirtieth day after the date of deposit with the Secretary-General of the United Nations of the twentieth instrument of ratification or accession.

2. For each State ratifying the present Convention or acceding to it after the deposit of the twentieth instrument of

ratification or accession, the Convention shall enter into force on the thirtieth day after the date of the deposit of its own instrument of ratification or accession.

Article 28

-1. The Secretary-General of the United Nations shall receive and circulate to all States the text of reservations made by States at the time of ratification or accession.

2. A reservation incompatible with the object and purpose of the present Convention shall not be permitted.

3. Reservations may be withdrawn at any time by notification to this effect addressed to the Secretary-General of the United Nations, who shall then inform all States thereof. Such notification shall take effect on the date on which it is received.

Article 29

-1. Any dispute between two or more States Parties concerning the interpretation or application of the present Convention which is not settled by negotiation shall, at the request of one of them, be submitted to arbitration. If within six months from the date of the request for arbitration the parties are unable to agree on the organization of the arbitration, any one of those parties may refer the dispute to the International Court of Justice by request in conformity with the Statute of the Court.

2. Each State Party may at the time of signature or ratification of the present Convention or accession thereto

declare that it does not consider itself bound by paragraph I of this article. The other States Parties shall not be bound by that paragraph with respect to any State Party which has made such a reservation.

3. Any State Party which has made a reservation in accordance with paragraph 2 of this article may at any time withdraw that reservation by notification to the Secretary-General of the United Nations.

Article 30

-The present Convention, the Arabic, Chinese, English, French, Russian and Spanish texts of which are equally authentic, shall be deposited with the Secretary-General of the United Nations.

IN WITNESS WHEREOF the undersigned, duly authorized, have signed the present Convention.

Convention on the Elimination of All Forms of Discrimination Against Men

The States Parties to the present Convention,

Reaffirming the goals set out in the Convention on the Elimination of All Forms of Discrimination Against Women,

Re-noting that the Charter of the United Nations reaffirms faith in fundamental human rights, in the dignity and worth of the human person, and in the equal rights of men and women,

Re-noting that the Universal Declaration of Human Rights affirms the principle of the inadmissibility of discrimination and proclaims that all human beings are born free and equal in dignity and rights and that everyone is entitled to all the rights and freedoms set forth therein, without distinction of any kind, including distinction based on sex,

Noting that both men and women have faced sex discrimination throughout history, only in different ways,

Further noting that, like women, men have also been the victims of harmful stereotypes,

Realizing that there will never be equality between men and women unless equality for men is also established,

Further realizing that in order to achieve actual equality between men and women, society will need to move away from traditional chivalry and toward actual equality,

Emphasizing that discrimination against men persists,

Recognizing that national governments and national courts, along with international courts such as the European Court of Justice, have recognized that examples of discrimination against men exist,

Further emphasizing that discrimination against men is just as wrong as discrimination against women and in the same vein, misandry is just as wrong as misogyny,

Understanding that societies need both men and women and that men and women need each other,

Further understanding that most men are honest, decent citizens and are not criminals, rapists, pedophiles, or violent in general,

Underscoring that consenting sexuality between adults is a normal and healthy part of human existence that is to be celebrated and that attacking it is counter-productive to bringing about equality between men and women,

Determined to bring about equality for men as well as women and, in doing so, create a better world for everyone,

Have agreed on the following:

PART I

Article 1

1. States Parties which recognize the 8th of March as International Women's Day are requested to recognize the 19th of November as International Men's Day.

2. States Parties which recognize an official Mothers' Day are requested to either recognize a Fathers' Day or to convert Mothers' Day into Parents' Day.

3. The existence of a Veterans' Day, though laudable, shall not be considered as an equivalent to a Men's Day.

Article 2

States Parties shall take all appropriate measures to eliminate discrimination against men with regards to military service obligations and ensuring that all military service obligations apply equally to women as well as men, in particular:

(a) Either repealing or rewriting to equally include women all military service laws which apply exclusively to men or even mainly to men, including laws whose implementation have been officially suspended;

(b) Either repealing or rewriting to equally including women all constitutional references to conscription which apply exclusively to men or even mostly to men, including such references which are not currently being enforced by law;

(c) Either repealing or expanding to equally include women any registration obligations regarding a potential future draft should such registration requirements apply exclusively or even mainly to men;

(d) Officially pardoning all men who failed to perform military service obligations, including registration failures, if such obligations applied at the time exclusively or even mainly to men;

(e) Passing legislation making it illegal to discriminate against men who failed to perform military service obligations (including registration obligations) which applied exclusively or even mainly to men at the time, in all areas, including but not limited to employment (both public and private sector), holding elected office, receiving grants and other scholarships, and receiving any other form of public assistance and/or benefits.

Article 3

States Parties shall take all appropriate measures to ensure that the lives of men are considered equally as valuable as the lives of women:

(a) States Parties shall take all appropriate measures to ensure that men have just as much right to be evacuated from war zones as women have (an exception can be made in cases of pregnant women and nursing mothers).

(b) States Parties shall take all appropriate measures to ensure that men's lives are considered just as valuable as women's lives in hostage situations (an exception can be made in cases of pregnant women and nursing mothers).

(c) While reserving priority space on lifeboats for children over adults would still be permissible, men must be given equal priority as women with regards to being evacuated from ships (an exception can be made in cases of pregnant women and nursing mothers).

(d) Men shall be evacuated from all other dangerous situations with equal priority as women (an exception can be made in cases of pregnant women and nursing mothers).

Article 4

States Parties shall take all appropriate measures to ensure that men are not discriminated against with regards to the distribution of international aid packages.

Article 5

States Parties shall take all appropriate measures to ensure that men's health is given equal priority to women's health, including in such areas as state funding for medical research.

An exception can be made in instances in which a State Party wishes to spend more research money on behalf of the sex with a lower life expectancy.

Article 6

States Parties shall also recognize that in many countries men have a much higher suicide rate than women and that measures need to be taken to address men's mental health.

Article 7

States Parties shall take all appropriate measures to ensure that societal pressures on men to not show their emotions be eliminated.

Article 8

States Parties shall take all appropriate measures to ensure that all social welfare services treat men equally with women and are just as available to men as they are to women.

Article 9

States Parties shall take all appropriate measures to ensure that blood feuds, especially those which apply to all male members of the family or any other group rather than merely towards the alleged culprit of the perceived injustice, be fully eradicated by fully prosecuting all of those responsible for perpetrating blood feuds.

Article 10

States Parties shall take all appropriate measures to ensure that the genital integrity of minor boys is respected equally to that of minor girls and that no form of genital cutting should occur on anyone, male or female, under the age of 18, or on any adult without the complete and total consent of that adult absent pressure from others.

Article 11

States Parties shall take all appropriate measures to ensure that any painful rite of passage ceremonies, especially those involving the cutting of the body, be eliminated, for both males and females.

PART II

Article 12

States Parties shall take all appropriate measures to ensure that men and women are charged the same rates of taxation.

Article 13

States Parties shall take all appropriate measures to ensure that all age requirements, in both the public and private spheres, apply equally to men as well as women, including but not limited to:

    (h) Retirement ages;

    (i) Minimum ages for withdrawing from pension funds;

(j) Minimum ages for collecting state benefits for the elderly;

(k) Minimum ages for marriage;

(l) Minimum ages for early release from prison for older people;

(m) Minimum ages for the buying, possession, and consumption of controlled substances such as alcohol;

(n) Minimum ages for entrance into business establishments.

Article 14

States Parties shall take all appropriate measures to ensure that any curfews apply equally to women as well as to men.

Article 15

States Parties shall take all appropriate measures to ensure that access to public transportation is never restricted to either women or men only.

Article 16

States Parties shall take all appropriate measures to ensure that no laws exist distinguishing between men and women with regards to the ability to drive a car, including but not limited to any restrictions on the time of day and the day of the week in question.

Article 17

States Parties shall take all appropriate measures to ensure that any and all civil service legal obligations such as jury duty apply equally to women as well as to men.

Article 18

1. States Parties shall take all appropriate measures to ensure that immigration policies apply equally to women as well as to men.

2. States Parties shall take all appropriate measures to ensure that all visa policies apply equally to women as well as to men in all respects, including but not limited to visa requirements, visa application forms, required documentation, and the obtaining of letters from the police ensuring that the applicant in question is a citizen in good standing.

3. States Parties shall not be allowed to deny entry into their countries of third country nationals based on sex.

4. States Parties shall not have asylum policies based on sex.

5. States Parties shall take all appropriate measures to ensure that fathers have the same rights of conferring citizenship on their children as mothers have.

Article 19

States Parties shall take all appropriate measures to ensure that any obligations that adult children have towards their elderly parents, whether legal or merely societal, apply equally to women as well as to men.

PART III

Article 20

1. States Parties shall take all appropriate measures to ensure that any hate speech laws which cover misogyny equally cover misandry.

2. States Parties which wish to consider hate speech laws as a violation of the concept of freedom of speech and therefore do not wish to have such laws shall not be discouraged from having such considerations.

Article 21

1. States Parties shall take all appropriate measures to ensure that society never loses sight of due process and that the rights of the accused, no matter how horrendous the accusations, are respected in all manners, including for such crimes as rape, pedophilia, and domestic violence.

2. States Parties shall take all appropriate measures to ensure that perpetrators of false accusations of all crimes, including rape, pedophilia, and domestic violence, are prosecuted to the fullest extent of the law.

Article 22

States Parties shall take all appropriate measures to ensure fairness with regards to domestic violence laws in that:

(a) Male victims of domestic violence are acknowledged by the state and that domestic violence against men is just as wrong as domestic violence against women;

(b) All the same resources available to female victims of domestic violence be made equally available to male victims.

(c) The perpetrators of domestic violence against men, be they male or female, be prosecuted just as vigorously as the perpetrators of domestic violence against women are prosecuted.

(d) All mandatory arrest laws vis-à-vis domestic violence must be repealed.

Article 23

States Parties shall take all appropriate measures to ensure that male victims of sexual assault are acknowledged by the state in that:

(a) All the same resources available to female victims of sexual assault be made equally available to male victims;

(b) The perpetrators of sexual assault against men, be they male or female, be prosecuted just as vigorously as the perpetrators of sexual assault against women are prosecuted;

(c) Made to penetrate is real and must be prosecuted as a form of rape like any other;

(d) Men should not be obliged to pay child support payments for children fathered from made to penetrate if these men do not wish to.

Article 24

1. States Parties shall take all appropriate measures to ensure that the law is enforced equally towards both female perpetrators as well as towards male perpetrators and that male perpetrators are not treated any more harshly than female perpetrators.

2. States Parties shall take all appropriate measures to ensure that incarcerated men receive the same privileges granted to incarcerated women, included visitation rights with regards to the prisoners' children.

Article 25

States Parties shall take all appropriate measures to ensure that policies, in both the public and private spheres (including but not limited to seating polices on airplanes), are neither written nor enforced in a manner that views all men as potential batters, pedophiles, or rapists.

Article 26

States Parties shall take all appropriate measures to ensure that pedophilia laws designed to protect minors are not used to prosecute them, in particular:

    (a) For taking and sending lewd pictures of themselves;

    (b) For engaging in sexual acts with each other provided that both minors are close enough in age to each other.

Article 27

States Parties shall take all appropriate measures to ensure that sex offender registries only include the names of perpetrators, both male and female, who are genuine threats to the community for such crimes as rape and pedophilia, and exclude the names of those convicted of crimes that are not a genuine threat to the safety of the community.

Article 28

States Parties shall take all appropriate measures to eliminate discrimination against men regarding safety policies, including in particular but not limited to:

    (a) Taxis shall not offer any discounts to women;

    (b) Subways and trains shall not have women only sections;

    (c) Institutions shall not be permitted to offer transportation to women only;

(d) Waiting rooms shall not be permitted to be for women only;

(e) Women shall not have the right to carry any weapons or any other forms of protection if men are not also permitted to carry such weapons;

(f) Parking spaces shall not be reserved for women only (an exception can be made in cases of pregnant women).

PART IV

Article 29

States Parties shall take all appropriate measures to eliminate all stereotypes and one-sided expectations regarding courtship and dating. Likewise, women shall be encouraged to make the first moves with regards to courtship and dating as well.

Article 30

1. States Parties shall take all appropriate measures to ensure that sexual harassment policies do not create an even more hostile environment, and that openness with sexuality, a sense of humor, and general friendliness are goals that society should have and should not be seen as examples of sexual harassment. Likewise, sexual harassment laws and policies should not hinder legitimate courtship or make it more difficult for men and women to work together.

2. The label of sexual harassment is to be reserved exclusively for truly egregious behavior in which the perpetrator intended to create an uncomfortable atmosphere and was fully aware that his or her actions were doing so.

3. States Parties shall take all appropriate measures to eliminate discrimination against men, both in the public and private sphere, regarding mandatory sexual harassment training seminars which are only required of men, as such a requirement constitutes discrimination against men. Likewise, States Parties shall recognize that women have also perpetrated sexual harassment.

4. Establishments, both public and private, which wish to eliminate their sexual harassment polices altogether shall not be discouraged from doing so.

Article 31

States Parties shall take all appropriate measures to ensure that all laws regarding sexual consent are reasonable, both in the manner in which they are written and the manner in which they are enforced:

(a) Affirmative consent policies shall not be considered as reasonable;

(b) While consent certainly can be withdrawn during the act of sexual intercourse, it cannot be retroactively withdrawn due to subsequent regret;

(c) Laws regarding the inability to grant consent based on intoxication shall apply equally to women as to men, so that a woman who has sexual intercourse with an intoxicated man would be just as guilty of rape as a man who has sexual intercourse with an intoxicated woman would be.

(d) Women who deceive men with regards to lying about birth control by doing things like lying about being on birth control pills or poking holes in condoms shall be considered as a failure to gain consent on the part of the woman. Such men shall be allowed to choose to refuse any custody and/or child support payments for any children conceived in such a manner.

Article 32

States Parties shall take all appropriate measures to ensure that sex workers are treated with the full dignity and respect which they deserve, including:

(a) A complete legalization and regulation of the sex trade amongst adults, both the buying and selling;

(b) Recognizing that consenting adults are entitled to engage in acts of sexuality with each other, even if consent was only granted for the want of money;

(c) Ensuring that the sex trade does not lead to human trafficking;

(d) Recognizing that adult pornography is a legitimate form of artistic expression and is protected by the concept of freedom of speech.

Article 33

1. States Parties shall take all appropriate measures to ensure the sanctity of marriage and that no policies be adopted to either discourage marriage or encourage divorce.

2. The existence of alimony payments is to be discouraged and kept to an absolute minimum.

Article 34

States Parties shall take all appropriate measures to recognize the important role that fathers play in the upbringing of children, and that no policies are adopted which discourage fatherhood.

Article 35

States Parties shall take all appropriate measures to eliminate discrimination against divorced men and non-custodial fathers, in particular:

(a) Joint custody shall be the default presumption;

(b) Claims made by fathers to child custody must be fully respected;

(c) Visitations granted to non-custodial fathers must be fully respected and mothers who disregard them must be held accountable and should perhaps have their custody revoked;

(d) Child support payments are to be for the exclusive benefit of the children in question and not the custodial parent;

(e) Child support payments must never be set at unreasonable levels and adjustments must be made for fathers who lose their jobs or who have taken a pay cut;

(f) Single fathers, including minors, should not be required to complete any parenting courses prior to gaining custody if the mother has no such requirement;

(g) Men shall have the right to request a paternity test and a man who has been found not to be the father of a child shall be allowed to terminate all custodial obligations, including financial ones, if he so chooses;

(h) States Parties shall take all appropriate measures to ensure that perpetrators of paternity fraud are prosecuted to the fullest extent of the law.

Article 36

States Parties shall take all appropriate measures to ensure that men are not forced to become fathers against their will:

(a) Men cannot be forced to donate sperm against their will;

(b) Men shall have the right to refuse custody/child support payments for children fathered thru stolen sperm;

(c) States Parties shall take all appropriate measures to ensure that stealing sperm is classified as a felony and is prosecuted as such;

(d) Men have the right to refuse to allow frozen embryos which they are the father of to be implanted should they change their minds in the meantime.

Article 37

1. States Parties shall take all appropriate measures to ensure that laws regarding spousal consent vis-à-vis vasectomies be identical to spousal consent laws vis-à-vis female sterilization.

2. States Parties which wish to allow for sterilization—both male and female—without spousal consent shall be permitted to do so.

PART V

Article 38

1. States Parties shall take all appropriate measures to eliminate discrimination against both men and boys

with regards to education, in particular, the awarding of scholarships or other grants for study.

2. States Parties shall recognize that in a number of countries boys have fallen behind girls academically at alarming rates and that measure must be taken to rectify this situation.

3. Laws and programs designed to advance girls' sports must not come at the expense of boys' sports.

Article 39

1. States Parties shall take all appropriate measures to ensure that any affirmative action programs, both in the public and private spheres and in both education and employment, be ended as soon as they are no longer needed.

2. States Parties which have minimum quotas for women in any given field, both public and private, must have the same minimum quotas in place for men.

3. States Parties which do not wish to bring about equality through affirmative action shall not be required to do so.

Article 40

States Parties shall take all appropriate measures to ensure that men are freely permitted to hold jobs that have traditionally been viewed as female, and that such men are fully accepted by society, and that businesses do not discriminate against men in the hiring for such jobs.

Article 41

1. States Parties shall take all appropriate measures to eliminate any harmful stereotypes against men who are stay-at-home-fathers and househusbands.

2. States Parties shall recognize that within the family, it is the children who are of paramount importance and that it is better for children to have one parent, either the father or mother, at home rather than being in a daycare center.

3. State Parties shall encourage men to take paternity leave.

4. State Parties shall encourage employers to offer fathers more flexibility with regards to working hours and leave of absences from work

5. State Parties shall encourage employers to be equally accepting of fathers who leave the workforce for a number of years as they are of such mothers.

Article 42

States Parties shall take all appropriate measures to eliminate discrimination against men by prohibiting business establishments from refusing to serve men, such establishments include but are not limited to hotels, restaurants, gymnasiums, and taxis.

Article 43

States Parties shall take all appropriate measures to eliminate discrimination against men with regards to the prices charged by business establishments in that men must always, including even in cases of special promotions, be charged the same prices as women in all sectors of the economy, including but not limited to, insurance, food and drink, admission fees, and airplane tickets. This article shall also apply to the public sector including but not limited to the charging of admission fees to things such as museums and public transportation.

Article 44

1. States Parties shall take all appropriate measures to ensure that businesses which have separate changing and showering facilities for men and women provide equal facilities to both men and women.

2. Ensuring that additional bathroom facilities are made available to women so that neither set of bathrooms has a longer wait time would not be in violation of this article.

Article 45

States Parties shall take all appropriate measures to ensure that special occasions such as weddings, funerals, and coming of age ceremonies which have traditionally not included both sexes equally should be modified in a way that they will.

Article 46

States Parties shall take all appropriate measures to ensure that in societies where women are permitted to wear dresses and skirts that go above the knee in businesslike settings in warm weather, should also permit men to not have to wear suits and even be permitted to wear shorts in such settings. For one thing, this would help men and women agree on air conditioning settings in offices on warm days.

My Modest Proposal

In the 18th century, Jonathan Swift wrote his famous essay, "A Modest Proposal." The purpose of this essay was to suggest various things the Britain could do to help Ireland, which at the time was under its dominion.

However, he began his essay in a humorous manner. He suggested that the best thing that the British could do for the Irish was to eat them! He made several arguments as to why that would be a good idea. I will never forget how my high school English teacher explained that by this point in the essay, you are either dying of laughter or are utterly horrified at his suggestion. Midway through the essay, he then states: "What I don't want, is for anyone to discuss with me, these alternatives," which is what he was really getting at. The rest of the essay consists of things that he thinks Britain should do to help Ireland.

Since so many feminists—and, to a lesser extent, women in general—think that the past was so oppressive to women and so favored men, let me make my own modest proposal: I say we bring the past back, only in reverse. As a result, yes, it is true that all positions of authority, such as judges and members of parliaments, will be women. Likewise, nearly all occupations, such as doctors and accountants, will be mostly or entirely held by women (possible exceptions might include men as secretaries or nurses, etc.). Depending on how far we go back, only women will be allowed to vote. Indeed, if we go way back, perhaps only girls will be educated.

However, at the same time, there will be a military service requirement for all girls upon coming of age. Depending on how far back we go, boys can either serve voluntarily or perhaps not at all. Likewise, in many countries, there will now be a higher retirement age for women. In life-threatening situations, such as sinking ships, priority will be given to innocent men and children. Chivalry will now dictate gentlemen first. From now on, women will have to make all the first moves with regard to dating. Furthermore, I wish to emphasize that when I mention that nearly all occupations outside of the house will be held by women, I was not just including white collar occupations: that will also include occupations such as coal miner, construction worker, etc. Their husbands will stay home and raise the children.

What's the matter? Doesn't this sound like an ideal arrangement for you women? No, well then, let's discuss the alternative: let's stop worrying about who had it worse (there were advantages and disadvantages both ways), and let's end all sexism: BOTH WAYS!!!

Chennai Train Rides and Their Implications

I am Dr. Carl Augustsson. I am the International Coordinator for the National Coalition For Men (NCFM), along with being the liaison contact for the Republic of Georgia. I am 44 years old. I have been a member of NCFM for over a decade now. However, my start in the Men's Rights Movement goes back much further. Back in January of 1989 (a month before I turned 12), I singlehandedly and without even the knowledge of my parents took action against my school in the United States on the grounds of sexism against boys. For the record, the investigation proved I was right.

In one sense, my involvement goes back a bit further, when, as a boy in the 1980s, I already began to make a list in my mind of all the injustices suffered by males around the world. The list now has about 40 items on it. I have turned this list into an international effort to get a global treaty on Men's Rights to complement, not replace, the already existing fabulous one on women's rights, a Convention on the Elimination of all Forms of Discrimination Against Men (CEDAM).

Needless to say, at this point in my life, I'd thought I'd seen it all with regard to sexism against males. At a minimum, I thought I had reached a point where nothing could shock me anymore. After all, what have I seen (or more accurately, know about): sexist conscription policies, circumcision, higher retirement ages for men (more on that in a minute), paternity fraud, false accusations of rape and domestic violence, men being screwed by the family court system, sexist funeral traditions here in the Republic of Georgia (I plan to write an essay about that in the coming months), and sadly so much more.

However, the recent report about the reopening of train services to the suburbs of Chennai, India really shocked me. For those of you who do not know, an article has recently gone viral (albeit from January) about the resumption of train services to the suburbs of Chennai, India. The policy (I am not sure if it is still in effect) was to restrict the train rides during peak hours (7-9:30 am and 4:30-7 pm) to women only. That's five hours out of the day. So if a man arrives at, say, 4:45 pm, he has to wait another 2 hours and 15 minutes in order to take a train. If he were a woman, he would not have to wait.

It astounds me that anyone could even dream up such a blatantly sexist policy. Worse yet, it could be implemented. If you don't have a problem with this, don't even complain about sexism EVER AGAIN! Obviously, such discrimination against any other demographic would never be tolerated. If such discrimination against men is allowed to stand, then there is no limit to what sexism against men is possible. Indeed, there have even been calls for curfews against men in both Britain and Australia. Moreover, it is shocking that there was so little outrage a decade ago over the t-shirt that read, "Boys are stupid; throw rocks at them."

This brings up the biggest reason (and there are many!) as to why I got involved with Men's Rights: even more than the many specific examples of sexism that I mentioned earlier, it's the attitude of society. We would never tolerate such blatant discrimination against any other demographic. Indeed, in some countries, people have been brought up on charges of hate speech for so much less (For the record, I am against that, as I firmly believe in freedom of speech). The good news is that if society could just show a similar aversion to discrimination against males that it shows towards every other demographic, most of these issues could be solved so quickly.

I mentioned the issue of higher retirement ages for men, in spite of the fact that men die younger. I am excited to announce that NCFM-Georgia will be filing a challenge with the Constitutional Court against the retirement age policy here in Georgia. For the record, it is 65 for men and 60 for women. A feminist here once told me that it is a matter of opinion as to whether that is sexism. No, it is not!!!

I still truly believe that an egalitarian world is possible and even within close reach, if we would just "go there."

An Open Letter to Feminism

If I were to write an ode to feminism, it would be entitled: to a movement I once admired. Perhaps I should mention a bit of my background. I was born in the late 70s in the US, with both US and Swedish citizenship. Generally speaking, I have been fairly conservative in my political and social views. I tend to support and believe in basic components of traditional Western society, such as the Christian faith, marriage and the nuclear family, free market capitalism, democracy, the rule of law, due process, etc.

However, if there was one aspect of traditional Western society that I did not like, it was traditional gender roles, along with uptightness with sexuality. Indeed, I have often called myself a "sex-positive Christian" or a "sex-positive conservative." Therefore, as a pre-teen in the late 80s, I looked up to feminism. After all, in my mind, you were the movement that was going to change the one aspect of traditional Western society that I did *not* like.

I could not have been more wrong about you. It turns out that you are actually the biggest sexists there are. If you really need examples, I could give them, but I think you know exactly what I am talking about. In terms of sexuality, you have, in many ways, created a neo-Victorianism while also promoting female promiscuity. On the one hand, you encourage openness with sexuality and mock religious conservatives as prudes, but God help the man who tells the wrong joke or makes the wrong pass to the wrong woman at the wrong time. As a result, the dating scene has been turned into a minefield. You then mock lonely men as "incels." Likewise, your attacks on pornography and prostitution are ridiculous. Indeed, the sex workers themselves don't like it either. So much for giving women choices. Could there be a more schizophrenic approach to sexuality than what we have seen from you?

Indeed, schizophrenia is all we have gotten from you. I realize that movements are often broad-based and with different wings, such as the men's rights movement, which I am a part of. However, that does not mean that movements can be all things to all people and/or two-faced. Feminism, are you Susan B. Anthony, or are you Andrea Dworkin? Pick one, as you can't be both. And once you have picked one, make it clear that the other is not welcome.

I am, however, going to give you a way out. As I mentioned, I am in the men's rights movement. Please believe me when I tell you that what first got me interested in this movement was not so much the damage of your excesses—which have been many and extremely damaging—but sexist injustices suffered by men, such as sexist conscription policies, or as I call it: the glorified national sexist enslavement of young men. You always claimed you had men covered, too. If so, please help me in my attempts to create a global treaty on men's rights (a CEDAM) to complement—not replace—the existing CEDAW for women.

An Open Letter to Women

I am a member of the much-maligned men's rights movement. However, would it surprise you that for a few years in my pre-teen/early teen years back in the late 80s/early 90s, I was a supporter of feminism? The reason? I genuinely believe in equality, and I thought that feminism did, too. Believe me when I tell you that many of us were strong supporters of having women in positions of authority. Indeed, many of us were proud of our countries for this.

I could not have been more wrong about feminism. It sadly turned out to be a sick, man-hating, anti-sex, anti-marriage, and anti-family cult.

There is so much I could say, but I will keep it concise. The main thing I would say is that it would really mean a lot to us if you could just understand that there are a number of disadvantages to being male and that it is long past time for women to acknowledge this. I could rest my entire case on sexist military service requirements, or as I call it, the glorified national sexist enslavement of young men. Please realize that in many countries such as Switzerland, Greece, and Finland, that is not just during wartime.

I think your problem is that you have no idea what it is like to be a man. I would suggest you read Norah Vincent's book "Self-Made Man" or simply watch her interview. The (female) reporter asked her if we know what it's like to be men. Her response: "We don't have a clue." Also, watch the movie "The Red Pill."

It seems like you really don't love us or empathize with us. Your claims that, of course, I love my father/brothers/husband/sons, etc., aren't enough. If anything, such claims seem a bit patronizing on their own. You need to also condemn the hateful rhetoric coming from feminism. You need to understand how difficult the dating scene is for younger men. You need to acknowledge all the positive things men have done for women throughout history.

I would like to close by saying that it breaks my heart to see so many men swear off dating and marriage, because I love the beautiful Western societies that our ancestors spend generations over the centuries building up. Indeed, I have citizenship in three different Western countries. I don't want to see them collapse.

We have a long and difficult road of healing ahead of us. Many men sadly think that it will be impossible. I still have faith, but you will have to make an effort yourselves and, for once, initiate something. To paraphrase the great 80s band REO Speedwagon: "I know it's not too late to turn around and get it straight. It's [our] fate to have you here with [us]."

Georgian Funerals

(I have purposely not included any names in this article. I hope none of the people mentioned indirectly get upset with me or feel that I have mentioned things that are too personal. I do not wish to offend anyone. Also, the events mentioned in this article are based on my recollection, and some of those mentioned in here may remember some of these instances somewhat differently. The reason I am mentioning personal experiences is because I found they would be the best way to illustrate my point. I have written a number of articles on men's rights and other issues I am passionate about in the past. However, I have never been as nervous about writing an article as I was when I wrote this article.)

I am Dr. Carl Augustsson. I am the head of the Georgian chapter of the National Coalition For Men (a men's rights organization based in the United States) and a proud Georgian citizen by marriage.

I have always been a firm believer in gender equality. Indeed, I even took action against my school at the age of 11 for sexism against boys. I have, therefore, always been aware that sexism against males is both real and just as wrong as sexism against females.

A number of years ago, I attended a funeral here in Georgia for the first time. I had never been to a Georgian funeral, so I had no idea what to expect. On the evening before the funeral, my wife told me that we would be going over to the house for a wake. She explained to me that usually, except for immediate family, the men stay outside. I remember thinking to myself that that seems so sexist, but I didn't say anything. I put a brave face on, but in realty I was quite angry. I remember thinking to myself afterward that while that was not right, at least it's over. The next morning shortly before we went to the graveyard, my wife explained to me that usually the men, besides immediate family, stand back. I thought to myself, not this sexism against men again! When we arrived at the graveyard, as I was starting to get out of the car, my wife suggested to me that I just wait in the car without even giving me a chance to respond (it was a cold, wet day in November).

As I was sitting in the car waiting, I found that I just could not contain my emotions anymore. I totally blew up when she got back to the car. I remember she said that now we would be going to the meal. My point was: we're going, or you're going?! When she told me that I would be going, I was actually not happy, as I had made up my mind while waiting in the car that I would rather not go anyway, just in case the meal also excluded men. Indeed, I was going to absolutely refuse to go. Thankfully, her younger sister was in the car and was able to talk me into going. My sister-in-law would later tell me that she had never seen me so angry before.

At the meal, she came up to me and asked me how I was doing. I was doing amazingly better since I wasn't hiding my real opinions anymore. She told me that she was so sorry and that she should have known how angry that was going to make me. She even told me that she felt honored the first time she was considered old enough to take part. And I asked her if she even thought about the part that if she were a boy that would not be happening. She answered that she probably would have since it was her grandfather, but at the same time, she admitted that that thought probably would not have crossed her mind.

I asked her if there would be anything else. She said "no," and even if there were, it would not exclude males. My point was: how do you know that?! "Why would it"? She asked. "Why would any of it"? Was my response.

A few years later, my father-in-law died while my wife and I were spending the summer in the United States with our children. Indeed, he died just before we were set to come back, so we could not make it to the funeral. However, we were at his grave for the 40-day ceremony. I was standing at the front, waiting for the ceremony to start. On several occasions, both my wife and her younger sister kept telling some of the people words like "don't" and "enough". I asked what was going on. They told me that everything was fine. (For the record, I have been slowly learning Georgian. Though I speak a number of other languages, this one has proven to be especially difficult for me).

After the ceremony was over, I heard some chatter. I heard my wife say that yes, he understands a fair amount of Georgian, but I don't think he is listening now. I turned and asked, what? They all laughed. My wife asked me to look around and see if I noticed anything. I did not. She then pointed out that I was the only male there. They explained that usually only close men like a husband or son come up. I asked what about son-in-law? They said maybe son-in-law. I pointed out that I am the son-in-law.

At that point, my wife mentioned what had happened the previous time and how I was going to refuse to attend the meal. At that point, my wife's cousin (who was the daughter-in-law of the woman who had died at the first funeral) turned to her and asked why I was going to refuse to attend the meal. After all, she never told me that I couldn't take part in the wake or ceremony. She then turned to me and told me that all I had to do was ask! After all, there were already three other males there, and I would have merely been the fourth. They all added that it was fine for me to be there. I thanked them for having me at the ceremony. I remember having an enjoyable conversation with the women there. Many of them agreed with me that husbands and wives should be next to each other in these moments. Also, many said that they would be so angry if the tradition were the other way around. Many also admitted to me that they had never even thought of that fact.

Likewise, they told me that they wouldn't mind if men took part in wakes. Indeed, I attended a funeral just a few months ago. I briefly took part in the wake until there were no more seats left. I am so glad that nobody seemed to mind me being there.

This brings me to a point I have wanted to make: how everyone here has been so accommodating to me here. It never ceases to amaze me how this fabulous country—and my wife's family in particular—has taken me in as an adoptive son. I remind myself every day how lucky I am.

A year later, at the one-year anniversary of my father-in-law's death, my parents were visiting Georgia at the same time. As the ceremony began, I wasn't sure if I would go up or stay back with my parents. I went partially up. In the middle of the ceremony, my father came up and mentioned that while not all the women went up, only women did. I explained that often, close men go up. Besides, the men aren't forbidden to go up; they usually don't. I added, by the way, nobody seems to know why it is this way. At the meal, my wife came up to me and said that all the women were wondering why I didn't come up. Indeed, they were even thinking about going back and getting me to show that it was ok, but they were worried that it would have embarrassed me. I told her to tell them that though I am, of course, not upset that they didn't get me, it would have warmed my heart if they had, and I am so grateful that they would think of me like that! Again, the kindness and hospitality here in Georgia never ceases to amaze me.

A year or so later, on what would have been my father-in-law's birthday, I went with my wife and her family to church, where the priest performed a small ceremony in my father-in-law's memory. Afterward, my wife's older sister made a comment about how I attend funeral services. My wife explained to me that usually, men don't attend these ceremonies either. I then reminded her about what she had said to me at the first meal, that there was nothing else after the meal, and that if there were, it probably would not exclude males. I asked her if she was still so sure of that. She admitted that, in all honesty, if there were something else, it probably would exclude males as well.

All of this brings up the question of why it is this way. At the first funeral I was at, my wife said she had no idea why it was this way. She suggested perhaps the men were being chivalrous. My response was, maybe if the women went first, but not if the men didn't go at all. After all, these wakes go on for hours, so there is plenty of time for everyone to have a turn. At the 40-day ceremony for my father-in-law, I asked if it was a privacy issue, and everyone said no. After all, men come in and give their condolences and there are often a few men. The biggest reason suggested is that perhaps since men are not supposed to cry, they stay back. If this is the case, then society needs to be far more accepting of men crying. One of the many reasons why I got involved in men's rights is because men need to be allowed to show their emotions, and society needs to accept and even encourage this. I would encourage all of you women to invite your men to fully take part in funeral services. Ask them, "Why are you staying out there? Come in!"

On a personal note, I have it in my will that I wish to be buried here. While I dearly love the other two countries in which I hold citizenship, I also dearly love this country that has taken me in, and I want my wife and I to be buried next to each other in the country of her birth. If I die, I ask that my funeral be based on equality. Please insist that the men fully take part. However, please do not exclude the women either, as that is not what I believe in. Furthermore, I wish to be buried wearing shorts. In the same manner, if my funeral is in warm weather, my guests will be strongly encouraged, though certainly not required, to wear shorts. There is no greater way to honor my life than to wear shorts! Finally, in the spirt of equality, I want a female tamada! For those of you unfamiliar with Georgian traditions, the tamada is the toast leader of the dinner, often at special occasions such as weddings, baptisms, and funerals.

  I truly believe that Georgia could become a model country with regards to gender equality. I plan to write another article soon explaining why that is. And from the sadness of funerals, can come the rebirth of an even better society based on love and equality between males and females.

Making the Republic of Georgia Ideal for Everyone

I am Dr. Carl Augustsson. I am the head of the Georgian chapter of the National Coalition For Men (NCFM) and a proud citizen of Georgia, the United States, Sweden, and, by extension, the European Union. In my previous essay about Georgian funerals, I mentioned that Georgia has the potential to be an ideal country with regard to both men's rights specifically and gender equality in general, and that's what I intend to explain here.

I want to begin by mentioning the positives with regard to men's rights here in Georgia. First of all, there is a major one: the fact in Georgia—like most European countries—the large majority of men (at least the Christian ones) are intact, i.e., not circumcised. Sadly—shockingly! —that is not the case in the United States. Perhaps I should give a brief historical overview. Up until the late 1800s, circumcision was just as rare in the US as in Europe. However, it started to catch on there and in other English-speaking countries due to the masturbation hysteria of the Victorian Era. Thankfully, this horrible practice has largely been dropped in other English-speaking countries, especially Britain and New Zealand. In the case of the United States, it's down to about half of newborn boys. By contrast, it was about 80% of newborn boys back in the 70s when I was born there. I consider myself to be incredibly lucky to be amongst the 20% who were not cut. Indeed, I have thanked my parents for this. I am confident that in another generation or so, the United States will retake its rightful place among the civilized countries of Western Civilization, where this practice is thankfully largely unheard of. There is, thankfully, a growing movement against this. Indeed, I have attended protests against it in the United States. This is truly the biggest national embarrassment that the United States has.

Another major thing to mention is weddings. Unfortunately, there are some people in some countries like the United States that think weddings should be all about the bride. Indeed, one person even told before me before my own US wedding (my wife and I had two wedding ceremonies: one in Georgia and one in the US) that as a groom, I didn't even matter. Part of the reason for this is that the bride's family traditionally pays for it. Thankfully, the US is slowly changing in this regard. It is so nice to see that here in Georgia, both families contribute to the wedding, and it is about both the bride and the groom equally. That is the way it should be in every country. It is shocking that anyone would disagree with that. Furthermore, I really like the sweet tradition here in Georgia of the bride's and groom's families paying for each other's wedding outfits.

One other positive thing to mention here in Georgia is that men are much more comfortable showing affection towards children. I have noticed that sometimes, when I took my young children into stores here, men would sometimes say hello to them and give them hugs. Sadly, in some countries, Britain in particular, men avoid all contact with children for fear of being accused of being pedophiles.

One positive trend I want to note is the growth in the number of men wearing shorts here in warm weather. Shorts are an important part of male liberation. Back when I first came here in 2001, and even when I started to live here in 2008, I was one of the few men wearing shorts. Today, it has become quite common. I like to joke to myself that I hope I had something to do with that!

Another reason Georgia could be made a model country with regard to true gender equality is that there is far less of the poisonous radical feminism that has sadly infected parts of Western Europe, North America, and Australia. It would be great if men's and women's rights advocates could work to together for equality. I have repeatedly stated that I am willing to meet with absolutely anyone on behalf of the National Coalition For Men. I have been honored to work with a battered women's shelter here in Georgia. We all need more of this.

An additional upside to the fact that there is far less radical feminist poison here is that the dating scene has not been turned into the minefield for men that it has in other countries.

At this point, I wanted to mention the biggest examples of sexism against men in Georgia. The biggest example is the sexist military service requirement. It is wrong to have a legal requirement for young men coming of age but not young women. This requirement must end. The second biggest example is the fact that men have a higher retirement age than women, in spite of dying younger. A feminist actually once told me that it is a matter of opinion as to whether that is discrimination. Obviously, she could not be more wrong. NCFM has filed a lawsuit against this law. More basically, society here, like in many places, needs to be more open with men showing emotions. Since I wrote extensively about the manner in which Georgian funerals exclude men in my previous essay, I will not repeat myself here.

One other thing I wish to mention: special holidays. Women have two holidays here in Georgia: Mother's Day and Women's Day, whereas men have none. There is now a movement to make the 19th of December Father's Day. That is fabulous. Let's also make November 19th Men's Day.

A side note about Men's Day: many people here wrongly tell me that Georgia used to have a Men's Day. What Georgia used to have was basically a Veteran's Day, which is fine, but don't dare call that a Men's Day. Instead, such a holiday is based on having a draft, the biggest example of a sexist injustice that men suffer around the world. In addition, why should Men's Day be based on one aspect of a man's life, whereas Women's Day is based on being a woman in general? I am so glad that I did not grow up with that day, as it would have been my least favorite day of the year. Indeed, imagine how upsetting it must have been for boys here to have girls congratulate them on a day based on the biggest injustice they were set to face in their lives, whereas the girls themselves did not have to worry about that. It was indeed a huge improvement for men that that day no longer exists. However, men here now need the 19th of November as International Men's Day.

I wanted to conclude by mentioning the global initiative that I have been working on for the past decade: a global treaty on men's rights (A Convention on the Elimination of all Forms of Discrimination Against Men, CEDAM) to complement, not replace the already fabulous existing treaty on women's rights, CEDAW. It would be fabulous if Georgia could sponsor this initiative at the United Nations.

Indeed, a few years ago, I gave a presentation on this topic at IBSU. I was so amazed at how well-received my topic was. Indeed, I was told how excited everyone was about it. I was quite nervous about submitting it. For those of you not in the men's rights movement, it can be shocking the amount of hate we get for simply saying: yes, gender equality is a fabulous thing; it just needs to include men as well. This is further proof that Georgia really can be the ideal country.

Together, let's all make Georgia ideal for everyone!

Military Conscription: Perhaps the biggest example of sexism in Western Civilization today

It must be stated from the outset that this article is purely against conscription and not voluntary military service. Voluntary military service can be a wonderful and fulfilling career. If you are a young man (or indeed a young woman!) who is considering a military career, you should definitely look into it, as a military career just might be perfect for you. Also, if you did voluntarily enlist in the military, don't you dare try to use the arguments in this article to justify desertion. Finally, to those of you who are defending or have defended your country, thank you for your service and your sacrifice!

Perhaps the greatest example of sex discrimination present in the world today is that of military conscription. How can a society claim to be in favor of sexual equality while only requiring men to do military service? The point of this essay is to argue against both conscription in general and—and probably more importantly—against the sexist nature of conscription laws. It must, however, be stated at this point that from a purely men's rights point of view, conscription is in and of itself acceptable, provided that the conscription laws apply equally to both men and women. Having stated that, most masculists, like me, favor the abolition of conscription altogether rather than expanding it to include women in order to right the sexist wrong of conscription policies as they currently exist in most of the countries that have them.

Let's not kid ourselves: conscription is a form of glorified slavery. For those who think that this is an overstated (or even offensive) comparison, realize that the definition of slavery is involuntary servitude, and that's exactly what conscription is. However, as was pointed out at the beginning of this article, military service is not in and of itself a bad thing, provided that it is done on a voluntary basis. In the same manner, slaves were often required to do farm work. Farm work is also not in and of itself a bad thing, nor is it degrading. Therefore, the objections to slavery were not over the fact that slaves were forced to do farm work; it was over the fact that they were not free to choose. The same thing is true with regard to military service; it's only a bad thing if it is forced onto people.

Numerous arguments have been made in favor of conscription. One of the more common ones is that it is necessary for the defense of the country. However, this mentality is a throwback to the First World War. Back then, warfare basically consisted of throwing a bunch of poorly trained conscripts into the trenches and counting how many were left at the end of the day. This occurred day after day until one side declared that it had had enough.

This is not, however, what modern warfare is all about. After all, while the threat of external invasion has not gone away altogether, today this threat is nearly gone from the world. Instead, the threat to national security comes either from internal insurrections (for example, from domestic terrorist groups like the FARC in Columbia) or from external terrorist groups. This threat requires—especially the external terrorist one—a small, highly trained group of elite soldiers who are capable of sneaking into a foreign country, destroying a terrorist cell, and sneaking back out before anyone realizes that they were ever there. Conscripts who serve for a year or less are incapable of such operations. Indeed, think of all the money that is wasted on training people who are already counting down the days until they can leave before they even arrive and leave the instant that they are allowed to, never to return. In an era when many countries are facing growing healthcare and pension expenses associated with an aging population, is this really the place where countries should be spending their money? Therefore, while there may very well be a few countries in the world that could claim that conscription is a necessary evil based on a national security argument, these countries are few indeed. And even in these countries, conscription is still an evil. As a result, these countries need to abolish conscription the absolute first instance that it becomes feasible. Moreover, if these countries truly need conscription, then it must be applied equally to women.

In addition to the national security argument, proponents of conscription have tried to make several other arguments in favor of its existence. The most common pro-conscription argument (after the national security argument) is that conscription is society's last chance to catch people who are on the wrong track and straighten them out. This argument is wrong for several reasons. First of all, it ignores the fact that prior to reaching draft age, people who need to have their lives straightened out have (at least until their mid-teens) attended (usually state-run) schools. Therefore, one institution—one that saw them over a number of years—failed to catch them and turn them around. If this failed to straighten them out, what's to say that the army will succeed? And if the army fails, then what?

Also, it must be remembered that there are plenty of criminals and drug addicts in countries in which military service is required. Indeed, many of these people completed their required military service, and still lead a life of crime or drug addiction. Moreover, this argument also ignores the fact that many conscripts found their military service experience—especially during a time of war—to be a very traumatic one, so much so that they later have trouble functioning in society. As a result, many turn to drugs or alcohol and/or join criminal gangs. In short, in this regard, conscription actually has the *opposite* effect.

Furthermore, this argument completely ignores the fact that this would require the drafting of "the many" in order to reach "the few". Besides, the type of people who are prone to a life of crime may very well prove to be the types who manage to get out of the requirement anyway. Finally, many—though not all!—of the supporters of this argument are against extending conscription to include women, and it is quite sexist to assume that there are no women in society who are on the wrong track and need to be straightened out.

Another argument—and an even worse one at that—in favor of conscription is that it is a rite of passage for young men into adulthood. First of all, no rite of passage should ever be legally required. Besides, do we really need a rite of passage at all, let alone one like this? And if a rite of passage into adulthood is needed, then why is there no female rite of passage?

One of the sillier arguments in favor of conscription is that it gives men positive experiences and skills for life. However, whether a man has positive experiences in his life is up to him. It is not the role of a government to ensure that its citizens have positive experiences in their lives. Are supporters of this argument suggesting that each country should create a "ministry for positive experiences"? Besides, this thinking totally ignores the fact that if these conscripts were not in the military, they would probably not be sitting at home and watching television all day. Instead, they would probably be out doing things such as studying, working, or travelling. Don't people have positive experiences from doing these things? Moreover, it cannot be ignored that many conscripts endure abuse and, in general, find military service to have been more of a negative rather than a positive experience in their lives. Finally, if military service is such a positive experience in the lives of conscripts, then why not extend it to women? After all, isn't a shame not to require women to have such a positive experience in their lives?

Another silly argument in favor of conscription is that it's great that everyone takes his turn defending the country. The alternative would be that only some do it. First of all, it was never *everyone*, as the law has always been sexist. Besides, while there is no doubt that society needs soldiers (and let's all be thankful that there are people in society who wish to be soldiers), it is also true that society needs doctors, nurses, teachers, firefighters, police officers, carpenters, electricians, factory workers, farmers, and several hundred more occupations. No one is ever legally required to have any of these occupations. Without just one of these occupations, society as we know it would not function. Is it not also true that only some perform these needed occupations?

However, just as the supporters of conscription have tried to make weak arguments in its favor, those of us who oppose conscription have been able to make stronger arguments against it. The strongest argument against conscription is also the most obvious: it is a legal requirement, and societies should always keep legal requirements to a minimum. Also, since it is a requirement, the likelihood of abuse at the hands of military officials is much stronger. There are two reasons for this. First of all, since the conscript does not have the ability to leave, he will basically have to just endure the abuse (more on this later). Secondly, since there will always be a steady supply of new recruits, military officials do not have to worry about stories of abuse driving away potential recruits. Also, one cannot ignore the fact that conscription interrupts schooling and careers. Moreover, it usually occurs right as young men are reaching adulthood when they should be out doing things like travelling and finding themselves. Finally, since so many of the recruits do not wish to be in the military and furthermore resent being there, they will only put in a minimal effort. Should the security of a country truly be based on large numbers of people who resent being in the military and can't wait to leave? Does that not just hurt the morale of the others there?

In addition to the arguments against conscription in general, there is also the fact that conscription laws have traditionally been sexist. Indeed, the modern state of Israel is one of the few (if not only!) places where women have ever been drafted. Even there the law is still sexist, as men have a three-year requirement, whereas women only have a two-year requirement. The sexist aspect of conscription has often, unfortunately, been overlooked whenever the merits—or, more accurately, the lack thereof!—of conscription are being debated. However, the time has long come to address the fact that conscription laws constitute one of the most (if not the most!) blatant examples of gender discrimination anywhere in the world today. How can societies which so claim to champion gender equality hold on to such an obvious example of sexism?

The good news is that conscription is on the decline worldwide. Indeed, in the case of Europe, the number of countries with conscription has gone from nearly all in 1994 to less than half today, with many of the countries that still have it either officially phasing it out or at least talking about phasing it out. As of now, only 14 European countries[1] still require military service with no plans to phase it out. These countries are Armenia, Austria, Belarus, Cyprus, Denmark, Estonia, Finland, Georgia, Greece, Moldova, Norway, Russia, Switzerland, and Ukraine. It is also important to note that some countries, like the Netherlands for example, never officially abolished conscription; they just stopped calling men up. Indeed, Dutch men are informed upon turning 17 that they have been included on an official conscription registry. While this definitely represents a huge improvement, it is still a sexist law that needs to be abolished.

In the case of Europe, citizens in member states of the European Union now have a powerful tool in the fight against sexist conscription laws. The EU has recently ratified the Lisbon Treaty, which is legally binding in all 27 member states of the EU. In several places, the Lisbon Treaty clearly states that there is to be complete and total equality between men and women. Likewise, the Lisbon

---

[1] It is surprising difficult to obtain information on which countries have conscription and which ones don't, as sources differ. These lists have been comprised after extensive searches of numerous sources.
Although it can be stated with near certainty that these lists are accurate, they may not be 100% accurate.

Treaty clearly forbids forced labor. Therefore, citizens in Austria, Cyprus, Denmark, Estonia, Finland, and Greece should now challenge conscription laws in court under the idea that they violate the Lisbon Treaty. After which, it should be made very clear to other countries such as Norway, Switzerland, Turkey, Moldova, and Georgia that they will have to abolish conscription if they ever wish to join the EU. Moreover, the Dutch (among others with similar situations) should also challenge their conscription on the grounds that it is sexist, even though it has been over a decade since anyone has been drafted in the Netherlands.

The abolition of conscription is not unique to Europe, as many of the countries of the Americas and other parts of the world have also abolished conscription in the same time period. In the case of the Americas, 9 countries: Bolivia, Brazil, Columbia, Cuba, El Salvador, Guatemala, Mexico, Paraguay, and Venezuela, still have conscription. In addition, the British territory of Bermuda also has conscription for its militia. As is also the case with Europe, a decade and a half ago, nearly all Spanish-speaking countries had conscription. However, it is important to note that as is the case with some European countries, some of the Latin American countries that have abolished conscription have not technically abolished it; they have merely stopped calling men up. Nonetheless, this still represents a huge improvement.

At this point, it is necessary to examine a few particularly egregious cases of conscription from around the world.

The first case to examine is that of Russia. Even though former Russian President Boris Yeltsin promised in 1998 that Russia would abolish conscription, this sadly has not occurred. Instead, the abuse of conscripts in Russia has become legendary.

The most dramatic example of this occurred on New Year's Eve in 2005, when a conscript, Andrei Sychev, was so badly abused that his legs and genitals had to be amputated. The Russian state did later prosecute those involved and paid for genital reconstructive surgery for the victim, but what little comfort that must have been (Source: http://www.theage.com.au/news/world/genital-rescue/2006/01/30/1138469635512.html).

Another outrageous example of conscript abuse in Russia is a scandal involving Russian conscripts allegedly sold as prostitutes. In addition, there have been convictions of officers for using conscripts as slaves. Needless to say: "the violent bullying…results in hundreds of non-combat deaths and suicides every year" (http://news.bbc.co.uk/2/hi/europe/4674366.stm).

However, the good news is that last year (2011), President Dmitry Medvedev was forced to acknowledge that conscription would have to be abolished in Russia. He stated that it would probably be sometime in the 2020s (Source:

www.strategypage.com/htmw/htatrit/articles/20110414.aspx). However, it may have to be sooner, as draft dodging has become rampant and is no longer seen as unpatriotic. Indeed, it is seen as a logical form of self-preservation in order to avoid abuse.

Another case to examine is that of Cyprus. What makes the case of Cyprus disturbing is the requirement that teenage boys (and young adult men, for that matter) obtain exit visas prior to leaving the country:

> It is extremely important for male visitors with parents of Cypriot origin to confirm their status as to completing **Cyprus Army Conscription** obligations. When you leave Cyprus, your documentation will be scrutinised at your departure point, and if you do not have the correct documentation, such as an **Exit Visa**, then you may be detained and not allowed to travel. (Emphasis in original)
> www.cyprusexpat.co.uk/article/id:2/cyprus-army--cyprus-army-service

Keep in mind that the above-mentioned requirement applies not only to Cypriot citizens but also to males who have a Cypriot parent. While such men could probably easily obtain such permits if they are not (and certainly have never been) Cypriot citizens, it is still an extra burden placed on men only.

One final case to examine is that of Singapore. Although this study has been mainly about Western countries, Singapore's enforcement of its conscription law is so draconian that it must be examined. For one thing, like Cyprus, Singapore also scrutinizes young men leaving the country in order to be sure that they are not leaving for the want of avoiding conscription. However, in the case of Singapore, there is an even more outrageous example: it is not even possible to renounce a Singaporean citizen until after having completed military service:

> In addition, for a male citizen, the government may withhold the registration of declaration of renunciation of Singapore Citizenship under Article 128(2)(b) of the Constitution of the Republic of Singapore, the provisions which are listed below:

> If the declaration is made during any war in which Singapore is engaged

>> Or

> If the declaration is made by a person subject to the Enlistment Act unless he has:

> 1. Discharged his liability for full-time service under Section 12 of the Act

> 2. Rendered at least 3 years of service under Section 13 of the Act in lieu of such full-time service

> 3. Complied with such conditions as may be determined by the Government

What this essentially implies is that if the male citizen is subject to the Enlistment Act and has not discharged his duty for National Service (or equivalent service), the Government has the right to withhold his renunciation of Singapore Citizenship. (www.guidemesingapore.com/relocation/citizenship/renouncing-singapore-citizenship)

This requirement is especially egregious. After all, if a man is so eager to avoid military service to the point that he is willing to give up his citizenship—knowing full well that he will have almost zero chance of ever getting it back—then by all means, he should be allowed to. How oppressive it is to force military service in such circumstances.

A Selective Service Registration

It must be stated that nothing in this sub-chapter should be seen as encouraging non-compliance with the law. If you are a young man turning 18 in the United States, complying with this unjust law is probably your best option. Failure to comply—though laudable—will probably only hurt you in the end. However, if you did fail to comply, realize that you did nothing wrong!

In the case of the United States of America, conscription has thankfully been far less common throughout the course of history than it has been in other Western countries. Indeed, it has not existed at all since January 1973. However, that unfortunately does not mean that there has been no sexist legal requirement for men with regard to the military in the United States of America. Instead, there is the unfortunate presence of "selective service registration." Within 30 days of turning 18, all men in the United States of America are required to register with selective service. This law even applies to all lawful permanent residents. Indeed, if a man becomes a lawful permanent resident in the United States prior to the age of 26 (at which point it is no longer possible to register) and fails to register, it is nearly impossible for him to ever obtain US citizenship.

Selective service registration was ended in 1975 by President Gerald Ford, two years after the military draft following the Vietnam War was abolished. However, in 1980, President Jimmy Carter brought it back in response to the Soviet Union's invasion of Afghanistan. Today, the Soviet Union no longer exists, and it is the United States of America that is now in Afghanistan. Therefore, the very reason given for bringing back draft registration is simply no longer valid. And yet, it lives on.

Not only has the reason for bringing registration back long ended—the Soviet Union pulled out of Afghanistan more than two decades ago!—it is obvious that bringing back draft registration did not serve its stated purpose, as it took the Soviet Union nearly a decade to pull out of Afghanistan. Clearly, this was not the reason that the Soviet Union pulled out of Afghanistan. And if it was the reason, then draft registration has long outlived its purpose. Besides, name one potential enemy of the US that is deterred by this system!

Not only is this registry totally irrelevant, it is also quite expensive. The US wastes over 20 million dollars a year on this (Source: the CATO Institute). While that may be a tiny amount of the overall budget, it is still a rather large sum of money that is being wasted, especially when one adds up the total amount over the last three decades. Think of what could have been done with that money. For example, that money could have been spent on hospitals for veterans. Besides, if such a registry were to ever be truly needed, think of how quickly and easily it could be started up again. There is, therefore, no reason to keep it on a continual basis.

As was stated previously in this section, it is nearly impossible to obtain US citizenship if a young man became a lawful permanent resident of the US prior to turning 26 without registering. However, the inability to obtain US citizenship is not the only thing that can happen to a man if he fails to comply. It is also nearly impossible to obtain a job with the federal government or many state governments. Such men are ineligible for all federally funded financial assistance to attend college. More recently, a majority of US states now require that men between the ages of 18 and 26 be registered in order to have a driver's license. Indeed, note the information contained on the Virginia Department of Motor Vehicle's website:

> If you are a male U. S. citizen living in the U. S. or abroad or a male immigrant (permanent resident alien)

residing in the U. S., and you are aged 18 through 25, you are required to register with the Selective Service System. With registration, you will be eligible for:

- Federal student loans and grants
- State student aid in the Commonwealth of Virginia
- Job training benefits
- Most federal jobs and jobs with the US Postal Service
- State jobs in the Commonwealth of Virginia
- US citizenship for male immigrants seeking citizenship

http://www.dmv.state.va.us/webdoc/general/sss.asp

First of all, note the poor punctuation with regard to spacing. Secondly, it is important to note that this information was not clearly posted on their website; it was necessary to search for it via the site map. Likewise, note how nowhere in the above-mentioned quote is there any reference to the fact that registration is unfortunately required in order for men between the ages of 18-25 to have a driver's license in Virginia. Both of those facts clearly indicate that even the government realizes that this sexist nonsense is nothing to be proud of. Most importantly, note how disingenuously the above-mentioned quote is worded.

It states, "With registration, you will be eligible for." While this statement may well be technically accurate, it is worded in an inaccurate and incredibly patronizing manner. After all, registration does not make a man eligible for any of the above-mentioned items; it is just that failure to register makes a man ineligible.

While there is no question that driving is a privilege and not a right, it still begs the question: what connection is there between compliance with a sexist law and the ability to drive a car? For that matter, what connection is there between registration and financial aid for college? The answer is simple: the authorities in the US don't have the courage to enforce this nonsense law. Indeed, since being reinstated in 1980 only 20 prosecutions have ever occurred, and none since 1986 (Source: http://hasbrouck.org/draft/prosecutions.html). As a result, the authorities have found a way to engage in "backdoor enforcement." Such a system is truly disingenuous. If a country is going to have an unjust law, then it should have the courage to enforce it. At a minimum, they should just let the law wither away and become more of a suggestion. The worst thing that a country can do is to create a backdoor enforcement system by making life difficult for those who fail to comply without actually prosecuting them. Indeed, by refusing to hire men who are at least 26 years old and failed to register, the government is, in essence, punishing these men for a crime for which they were never even charged, let alone convicted.

In order to further encourage compliance, the US government has been running a series of irritating and, quite frankly, insulting radio commercials to encourage registration. In one commercial, a father tries to have a conversation with his son about life's important topics. One of the topics he tries to discuss with his son is about girls. If he wants to talk to his son about girls, he should mention that they are privileged not to be affected by this sexist, useless law. The commercial ends with the announcer mentioning that you (a reference to parents) may have to repeat your message. How sexist and insulting to assume that teenage boys are stupid and have to have things told to them several times in order to understand!

Even more infuriating than this commercial are the ones in which women are telling men about the importance of registering. In one such commercial, a woman talks about how much she respects men who register and that we must all do our part to keep the United States safe. First of all, her "respect" is neither needed nor desired. Second of all, she mentions that we must *all* do our part to keep the US safe. That begs the question, what is her part? Basically, her part is getting paid to voluntarily do a radio commercial. Such women should be considered as anti-male. If nothing else, nobody likes to be patronized, and her claim that she "respects" men who register is incredibly patronizing.

What is also infuriating about commercials using women to promote this sexist law is that the US government is clearly trying to use female sex appeal to reach young men. This begs the question: where are the feminists on this? Are these not the same feminists who always become so livid any other time that female sex appeal is used to get the attention of men? Finally, imagine men being used in a commercial to promote a legal requirement that affected women only, not that such a requirement would ever be allowed to exist, nor should it.

Instead of being called "selective service," this nonsense should be known as "sexist service," or perhaps "selective equality." Indeed, feminists who claim to believe in equality but who have no objection to the blatant sexism in this law are guilty of believing in "selective gender equality."

However, rather than extending this law to include women, the best thing to do is to simply abolish it. After all, if the attacks of September 11, along with the subsequent wars in Afghanistan and Iraq, did not necessitate the need for a draft—and they didn't!—then clearly nothing will. In addition, the records need to be destroyed, and no one should ever be required to state whether he complied with this sexist law.

B Military Conscription and the False Argument of Pregnancy

Some have tried to justify the sexist laws with regard to conscription with the argument of pregnancy. The argument is that since only women have pregnancy, it is acceptable to require military service of only men. These people believe the conscription polices of their respective countries are fair because: "women have pregnancy and men have the military."

This argument is absurd for a number of reasons. First of all, there is the obvious fact that pregnancy is a choice, whereas military service is a legal requirement; how can a choice be compared to a legal requirement?! After all, women can choose to serve in the military and never be pregnant. By contrast, women can choose to have children and never serve in the military. Likewise, women can also choose to do either both or neither. Therefore, women have four options, whereas men have one legal requirement. Is this equality? Moreover, the supporters of the pregnancy argument need to be asked a simple question: if you think that it is fair to only require military service of men because women have pregnancy, then do you think that countries that don't require military service of men are being unfair to women? After all, based on that thinking, women still have pregnancy, whereas men have nothing. If the answer to this question is no, then how can both systems (requiring military service of men versus not requiring military service of men) be fair to both men and women?

Supporters of this argument point out that societies need to repopulate themselves, just as society needs to defend itself. However, while this point may seem logical at first glance, a closer inspection soon reveals that the mindset behind it is flawed. While it is true that societies need to repopulate themselves, that does not mean that there is a connection between this and the need that societies have to defend themselves. After all, would it be wrong for governments to levy higher taxes on men so as to pay for the health care costs associated with pregnancy? This example would actually constitute a stronger connection between pregnancy and a sexist law that goes against men.

However, this would also be ridiculous because—if for no other reason—it is a myth to believe that there is a connection between a specific tax and a specific budgetary expense. After all, in the end, all money collected in taxes merely goes into the government's coffers. There would, therefore, be no more connection between an extra tax on men and healthcare costs associated with pregnancy, as there currently is no connection between pregnancy and conscription. Since we all recognize the absurdity of the example of charging men extra taxes to pay for pregnancy-related healthcare costs, can we not all now see the absurdity of the pregnancy argument with regard to justifying sexist conscription laws? Moreover, can we not all now also see how dangerous this pregnancy argument is in that it could be used to justify *any* discrimination against men? In addition, under this thinking, could a government also *require* pregnancy of women? After all, societies need to repopulate themselves.

Likewise, failure to perform military service is often seen as unpatriotic. Is it, therefore, also true that women who refuse to have children are also unpatriotic? Also, if a man who is still young enough to perform military service were to apply for foreign citizenship, he would often be expected to perform military service for his adopted country. This often even applies to men who aren't citizens but merely permanent residents. By contrast, if a woman of childbearing age were to apply for foreign citizenship, would the immigration officials ask her how many children she plans to have? Such a question would, understandably, by quite offensive. However, asking young men whether they would be willing to perform military service should be seen as equally offensive. It must also be mentioned that there are cases of women who have dual citizenship, whereas their brothers do not, simply because their brothers are unwilling (as are their sisters!) to perform military service. Is this fair? After all, many of these women will never be pregnant.

Moreover, should men who promise never to cause pregnancy—even to the point of getting vasectomies—be exempt from conscription? After all, if it is possible and acceptable for women to never be pregnant and never be in the military, then why can't the same thing be true of men?

Besides, while it is true that only men have military service, it is not entirely true that only women have pregnancy when one considers the fact that women understandably expect their husbands to look after them during their pregnancies. Indeed, it is the responsibility of men to care for the mothers of their future children during pregnancy. However, do these same women look after their husbands while they're in the military by doing things like helping them to clean their barracks or bringing them water when they need it? Indeed, while pregnancy (for the most part) requires a woman to have been with a man and therefore gives her a man who can be reasonably expected to care for the mother of his future child, military service does not require a man to have a woman who could potentially look after him. Moreover, even if these women wanted to assist their husbands/ boyfriends during military service, they wouldn't even be permitted to do so. Therefore, in this sense, men even have pregnancy—albeit at a much-reduced level—whereas women still do not have military service at all.

Finally, it must be remembered that being pregnant, giving birth, and breastfeeding give mothers a special bond with their children that fathers will never have. Likewise, while women are always certain as to how many children they have and as to whom their children are, this is not the case with men. It is not uncommon for men to discover that their children really aren't theirs or to discover years later that they had children that they were unaware of and, therefore missed out on raising. As a result of these facts, many men actually consider the fact that pregnancy applies to women only to be a disadvantage for men. In short, this is a ridiculous argument in favor of sexist conscription policies on so many levels.

C Conclusions

Make no mistake about it: conscription is the glorified national sexist enslavement of young men. As a result, it is truly an abomination. It is sad that such an abomination could be permitted to exist in the 21st century. If you are a man who avoided conscription—even to the point of violating the law—realize you did nothing wrong. Moreover, you did not disgrace your country. Instead, your country disgraced you! Indeed, shame on your country! If you violated such a law, that should not be held against you since you should have never been placed in that position to begin with. Indeed, people who avoid sexist conscription laws should be considered in the same manner in which society views people who escaped from slavery. However, it is also very important to note that if you are a man who served as an unwilling conscript, you should never be considered a traitor to the cause of men's liberation. Instead, thank you for your service to your country, even though it was wrongly forced on you against your will.

As for previous time periods, perhaps the case can be made that conscription was a necessary evil. After all, throughout history, it was basically a case of conquering or being conquered, creating an empire, or becoming a part of someone else's empire. In such an environment, perhaps societies sadly had no choice but to require military service. Furthermore, the fact that it only affected men was understandable, as in the past, only men were in the military, and only men administered governments. After all, no one was claiming in past centuries that gender equality was a good idea. Indeed, in the past, very few would have even suggested such a concept. However, it's now the 21st century! Both gender roles and conscription have long become dated concepts, and thankfully so. As was stated earlier, the good news is that conscription is on the decline throughout both Western civilization and the world as a whole in general. Furthermore, attitudes towards conscription in many societies have been changing over the last couple of decades, as many people have thankfully come to realize just how horrible conscription is. It can be stated with confidence that it is now only a matter of time until more—and hopefully, someday all—countries abolish conscription.

However, if societies insist on both keeping conscription and keeping it sexist, then perhaps this small proposal could be adopted into law: that only men be allowed to enforce conscription laws. After all, if the law only affects men, then does it not make sense that only men enforce it? Furthermore, it is infuriating to see women enforcing sexist laws against men. Therefore, only male police officers should be allowed to arrest men for conscription violations, and only male judges should be allowed to hear such cases. This proposal, by the way, extends to selective service registration in the US. Indeed, selective service should adopt an official policy of hiring men only.

Another small proposal for societies that insist on keeping sexist conscription laws: such countries should give military veterans extra consideration when applying for government jobs. Indeed, it is already this way in the United States. However, the US military has been an all-volunteer force since 1973. Such policies are good, as societies should always give back to those who are willing to defend them. However, in countries with general sexist conscription, if such a policy were to be adopted, feminists would almost certainly immediately view this as being an unfair advantage for men, never mind that the legal requirement is and always has been extremely unfair to men. That, however, is sadly of zero concern to feminists, in spite of their erroneous claims that they believe in gender equality.

In the end, if societies truly wish to embrace the concept of gender equality—which every society should—then conscription laws that apply to men only can no longer be allowed to exist, as this is a huge contradiction. As the expression goes, if it walks like a duck and quacks like a duck, then it's a duck. Therefore, if it walks like discrimination quacks like discrimination, then it *is* discrimination. This is not just discrimination but one of the biggest (if not *the* biggest) examples of discrimination in existence. Likewise, as has just been shown, the pregnancy argument is completely invalid and cannot be used to justify this sexist double standard. If you are a woman who supports sexist conscription laws, then you should be considered anti-male. And if that's a little harsh, then remember, it is easy to glorify a concept that does not affect you. To all of you women who agree that this is sexist and wrong, your support is truly heartwarming. The good news is that this dilemma (the concept of gender equality alongside a sexist conscription policy) has a very easy solution: simply abolish conscription. Problem solved!

However, at this point, it is not enough to merely abolish conscription. It is also necessary to pardon all men who have been convicted of draft dodging since their only crime was avoiding a sexist and, therefore, unjust law. The same thing should also be true for men who did things like renounce citizenship or had themselves declared mentally insane in order to avoid conscription. These men should now be allowed to come forward and have these things reversed. In order to back this up, laws making it illegal to discriminate against those who avoided conscription also need to be passed. Likewise, constitutional guarantees should be passed to ensure that this never happens again. Finally, an official apology needs to be issued.

Sources:

The Age: http://www.theage.com.au/news/world/genital-rescue/2006/01/30/1138469635512.html

The BBC: www.bbc.co.uk

The CATO Institute: www.cato.org

The CIA World Fact Book: www.cia.gov/library/publications/the-world-factbook

Cypriot Expat: www.cyprusexpat.co.uk/article/id:2/cyprus-army--cyprus-army-service

Department of Motor Vehicles, Virginia: http://www.dmv.state.va.us/webdoc/general/sss.asp

The European Union's homepage: europa.eu

Guide Me Singapore: www.guidemesingapore.com/relocation/citizenship/renouncing-singapore-citizenship

Hasbrouck.org: hasbrouck.org/draft/prosecutions.html

Nation Master: www.nationmaster.com

The New York Times Blog: http://thelede.blogs.nytimes.com/2007/02/13/russian-soldiers-sold-for-sex/

Selective Service System: www.sss.gov

Strategypage: www.strategypage.com/htmw/htatrit/articles/20110414.aspx

The United States State Department's homepage: www.state.gov

War Resisters' International: http://wri-irg.org

Sexköpslagen

*I wish to strongly emphasize from the outset that this article is purely about **adult** prostitution. Nothing written here is to imply any support whatsoever for child prostitution.*

In 1998, Sweden passed a law called "sexköpslagen," which roughly translates to "law on the buying of sex." Under this law, the buying of sex is a criminal offense, but the selling of sex is not. What is worse is that this nonsense law has been copied in both Norway and Iceland. In fact, the Norwegian law is actually far worse. Under Norwegian law, a Norwegian who travels to, say, the Netherlands or Germany, where prostitution is legal, and has sex with a prostitute, could be arrested upon returning to Norway. The supporters of this provision said that they wanted to stop "sex tourism." My response would be: none of your business! Why people choose to travel is not for the government or activists to worry about.

The thinking behind sexköpslagen was that the prostitutes were being exploited. They, therefore, should not be arrested. Furthermore, the thinking was also that the prostitutes were being exploited by the men who visited them.

Both this law and the thinking behind it are so wrong that it is hard to even know where to begin. First of all, consenting adults should be allowed to buy and sell sex from each other. Also, does it not seem wrong that the party that is making money in the transaction is not committing a crime, whereas the party that is paying is?

In addition, supporters of this law seem to have totally ignored the fact that, in many instances, prostitutes have been known to aggressively pursue single men that they encounter on the street. Indeed, those of us who have travelled and lived in Eastern Europe could certainly attest to that. With this fact in mind, it is totally wrong for someone to legally pursue a potential customer who would, in the end, be committing a crime, while the pursuer would not only not be committing a crime but would also be making money in the process. Moreover, how can men who give into the aggressive pursuits of prostitutes be seen as exploiting them? Indeed, could pushy prostitutes actually be seen as exploiting men? While such aggressive prostitutes are rare in Sweden, the supporters of this law—if asked— would almost certainly want to see it replicated around the world, including in countries where pushy prostitutes are common. It is worth repeating a quote from a Swedish prostitute in a BBC article about this law: "I mostly work in high luxury hotels and apartments. I don't feel used. Sometimes I feel I'm using them" www.bbc.co.uk/news/world-europe-11437499, September 30, 2010.

It must also be remembered that while the prostitutes may not be committing a crime, they still have to hide their activity in order to protect their clients. While the supporters of this law could easily point out that the law does not forbid women from selling sex, it still requires them to sell it to people who are breaking the law. Furthermore, if a woman—or man!—wishes to sell sex for money, then what right does the government have to say no? Therefore, if the thinking is that it should be their right to sell sex, they should not be forced to sell it to people who are breaking the law.

However, it is very important to note that even though selling sex is not a crime in Sweden, the intention behind this law was for prostitution to come to an end. In the same BBC article, the Detective Superintendent of Stockholm's Police Surveillance Unit stated, "[i]t should be difficult to be a prostitute in our society—so even though we don't put them in jail, we make life difficult for them" www.bbc.co.uk/news/world-europe-11437499, September 30, 2010.

As has been previously stated, the prostitutes themselves do not like this law. Many feel that far from protecting them, it harms them both by stigmatizing their work and by making them hide it. As a result, the Rose Alliance, an organization representing Swedish prostitutes, lists the abolition of **sexköpslagen as point 3 on its platform: "Ett avskaffande av sexköpslagen...Detta som ett första steg mot en total avkriminalisering av sexindustrin."**
www.rosealliance.se/?s=sexk%C3%B6pslagen.
Translation: "an abolition of sexköpslagen...That is a first step towards a total decriminalization of the sex

industry." Moreover, the prostitutes themselves claim that the law has made working more dangerous for them. In short, if the law was intended to help prostitutes, it has failed miserably. Likewise, as if often the case with such activism, the people that the activists are allegedly helping don't even want this help. Indeed, to what extent are feminists actually exploiting prostitutes for the want of a political agenda? Now, who's exploiting prostitutes?

It must also be remembered that if prostitution is to be considered a crime, it is strange that buying is seen as so much worse than selling. After all, in the case of drugs, it is the other way around. While both the buying and the selling of drugs are illegal, it is the selling of drugs that is the far more serious crime.

As for the argument that it is the men who go to prostitutes who are creating a demand for prostitution, the same thing is also true with regard to drug dealing: if nobody bought drugs, there would be no drug dealers. Besides, the demand for prostitution is simply a part of the desire for sexual fulfillment, which is a normal and even healthy part of human existence. This demand is, therefore, not in and of itself a bad thing, provided that it is done respectfully. Indeed, the fact that feminists are against adult prostitution is based on the fact that they are uncomfortable with male sexuality in general. In fairness, it must be pointed out that this law is not sex-specific. Therefore, a woman going to a male prostitute (as an increasing number of women are) or a homosexual going to a prostitute of the same sex would be just as guilty under the law. However, it is obvious that that was not what the authors of this law had in mind.

One other important point on the causes of the demand for prostitution: we must not forget that a lot of the demand for prostitution may very well be caused by the fact that dating has become more difficult thanks to the very feminists who so hate prostitution. Therefore, to what extend do the actions of feminists create more of a demand for prostitution?

In short, either prostitution is a crime, or it isn't. Ideally, it would not be seen as being a crime. However, if it is a crime, then everyone involved should be considered to be breaking the law. Punishing one side only is fundamentally wrong.

It is especially sad to see a country such as Sweden, which used to be so open with sexuality, become so uptight. What is worse is that there is a real risk of this nonsense, double-standard law spreading to other countries, as it has already spread to Norway and Iceland. Indeed, there is already concern that if the opposition Socialists come to power in the next election in Denmark, they might try to pass a similar law in Denmark. That would be strange when one considers the fact that it was the Socialists who legalized prostitution in Denmark back in the 1990s when they were last in power.

A large part of the reason that this law—flawed as it is—could spread is that such politically correct causes often turn into bandwagons. Once such politically correct bandwagons begin, people sadly become too afraid to speak out against them. Worse yet, people often feel the need to express their support for such concepts, even if they secretly do not like them. Many supporters of this law in Sweden claim that prostitution is inconsistent with the concept of gender equality. Openness with sexuality is not inconsistent with gender equality. If anything, the exact opposite is true.

There is a good chance that the Nordic region will rediscover its historical tolerance of sexuality and that this ridiculous law and the mentality behind it will have merely been an anomaly at one point in time. Indeed, as a Swedish citizen myself, I used to be so proud of Sweden's openness with sexuality. Like me, the Nordic region, in general, often has—and rightfully so—been proud of its openness with sexuality. Nonetheless, there is no guarantee of this. Those of us who value both gender equality and sexual freedom must confront this political correctness.

On the Notion that Legal Sex Work Leads to Trafficking

Nearly a decade ago, I wrote an essay against the so-called "Swedish Model" of prostitution, which bans the buying but not the selling of sex. I, therefore, do not wish to rehash the arguments made in that article. I will just say that while this model has sadly since spread to other countries such as Canada and Ireland, it has not spread as fast as the proponents would have liked. Indeed, it will hopefully be peaking soon.

Part of the reason that it may be peaking is that the case against sex work, in general, is such a weak one. Basically, if consenting adults wish to buy and sell sex from one another, why should they not be allowed to? The reason is that there are a number of moralists, both Christian conservatives on the right and feminists on the left (in what is truly one of the most unholy alliances ever), who are uncomfortable with sexuality in general.

However, many of those in both groups probably realize the inherent weakness in arguments based purely on sexual morality. They have, therefore, turned to what would be a stronger argument: sex trafficking. After all, those of us who believe that consenting adults should be allowed to buy and sell sex from each other will not be persuaded by moralistic arguments. However, some of us could be convinced to ban sex work if we could be convinced that it leads to human sex trafficking. This would, therefore, be the moralists' strongest argument, even if their opposition is based mainly on their moral objections. It is, therefore, not surprising that many of them are making this claim.

This, however, begs the question: is it true? We have often seen in politics where a group of people are willing to make false arguments to bolster what is otherwise a weak case (and arguing that consenting adults should not be allowed to buy and sell sex from each other is indeed a very weak case). It is the purpose of this short article to explore whether this is the case.

It must be pointed out that hard figures can be a bit hard to come by. Likewise, a number of studies and articles on this topic have already been written. I will, therefore, merely provide a brief summary. For a fuller discussion, one can click these links and read the full studies.

'End demand for prostitution' approaches have been most heavily promoted by prostitution abolitionists, who claim that penalising sex workers' clients will help fight trafficking. Sex workers' rights groups and some antitrafficking organisations (including GAATW) have strongly opposed criminal penalties against clients as this approach:

• Has not reduced trafficking or sex work;

• Threatens sex workers' income security and working conditions, such as by increasing competition amongst sex workers and increasing the vulnerability of sex workers who must negotiate with nervous and scared clients (i.e., less time for workers to determine whether a potential client is safe or not);

• Has not stopped violent or abusive clients who are more experienced at evading law enforcement, but has ended up impacting less experienced clients and 'good' clients;

• Dismisses and silences the concerns, priorities, and knowledge of sex workers;

• Muddles anti-trafficking efforts by confusing trafficking with sex work;

• Increases police's power over sex workers; and

• Increases stigma against women in sex work.

(https://www.gaatw.org/publications/MovingBeyond_SupplyandDemand_GAATW2011.pdf?fbclid=IwAR2JkgloR0VFOSTnU5hw-2XCvoZ4sxcJorJxTXV-wlaKoFoWYChqBBLv5rw)

"Australia's anti-trafficking laws have resulted in thousands of raids, resources devoted to surveillance and investigations, but have found very little evidence of trafficking," Elena Jeffreys, President of Scarlet Alliance, said today. "The Police found what sex workers always knew; trafficking-like work conditions in Australia are rare. All evidence and research backs up this conclusion." (http://www.scarletalliance.org.au/media/News_Item.2011-10-10.4626/view?fbclid=IwAR10IlgQAydOCOB95ll7W0UUk0xlrUiUT1y8V6OrL1jcWmq4n6uRMZFyD0)

Other articles have been written about instances where the police in other countries such as Britain, hearing about sex-trafficking being out of control, searched brothels across the country and could not find a single woman who was there against her will or who had been brought into the country under false pretenses.

In short, research has shown that criminalizing sex work does not lead to a decrease in sex trafficking. Instead, if it has any effect, it merely creates more problems.

Above all, it is important to remember that even if legal sex work leads to sex trafficking, that does not mean that it should be illegal:

> It would be nonsensical to abolish all forms of garment manufacturing in which people are trafficked; rather, states must monitor recruitment practices, protect labour rights of garment workers, and ensure occupational health and safety and like measures. (https://www.gaatw.org/publications/MovingBeyond_SupplyandDemand_GAATW2011.pdf?fbclid=IwAR2Jkg1oR0VFOSTnU5hw-2XCvoZ4sxcJorJxTXV-w1aKoFoWYChqBBLv5rw, p23)

Even more importantly, we must remember that even if it were 100% proven that legal sex work does not lead to any trafficking whatsoever, the prostitution prohibitionists would not be persuaded, as this is not the source of their opposition anyway. In the end, probably the most important point in all of this is the fact that the prohibitionists have routinely ignored and dismissed what the organizations representing sex workers think. If there is anyone we should be listening to, it is them.

One final note about the absurdity of criminalizing consensual sex work that appeared as a Facebook meme in 4 frames, with a man talking to a woman with a police officer behind them. In the first frame:

Man: Can I give you money?

Woman: Of course!

In the second frame:

Man: Can we have sex?

Woman: I guess

In the third frame

Man: Ok, I will give you the money for the sex

Police Officer: Hold on, that's illegal!

In the fourth frame:

Man: To make a movie, which I will sell and keep the profits for myself

Police Officer: Oh sure, you can do that. Why didn't you say so?!

I would like to Thank the Rose Alliance, the organization that represents Sweden's sex workers, for helping me with this article.

The Supplemental DS-157 Nonimmigrant Visa Application Form

With the 10-year anniversary of the horrible attacks of September 11th right around the corner, I decided to write an article about one of its effects: the introduction of the Supplemental DS-157 Nonimmigrant Visa Application Form. The existence of the Supplemental DS-157 form for nonimmigrant visa applications to visit the United States of America so outraged me that I decided to dedicate an entire chapter in the book I'm writing about the Men's Movement to it.

Following the attacks of September 11, 2001, on the United States of America, the United States government introduced the Supplemental DS-157 visa application form. What is infuriating about this form is that it is required of all male applicants between the ages of 16-45. For citizens of four countries that are considered to be state sponsors of terrorism: Cuba, Iran, Sudan, and Syria, the form is required of all applicants over the age of 16.

To quote the webpage of the State Department of the United States of America:

> A Supplemental Nonimmigrant Visa Application, Form DS-157, provides additional information about your travel plans. Submission of this completed **form is required for all male applicants between 16-45 years of age. It is also required for all**

applicants from state sponsors of terrorism age 16 and over, irrespective of gender, without exception. [Emphasis in original] (http://travel.state.gov/visa/temp/types/types_1262.html)

While this form may look rather innocuous at first, as it is only on page long, it actually can be a long form to fill out. The reason is that some of the questions, depending on the life experience of the individual, are quite long. One such question (Question 9) is the requirement of listing every country visited in the last ten years, including the year in which these countries were visited. For those of us who travel the world frequently, that is a difficult question to answer. For such people, the answer could easily include over 50 countries, many of which have been visited several times over the last ten years.

Another difficult question (Question 17) to answer is to list all of the schools and universities attended, excluding elementary schools. This would not in and of itself be bad were it not for the fact that these young men are also required to list the addresses and telephone numbers of all of these institutions. This can be a tedious and time-consuming process. What is obvious here is that they are trying to see whether the applicant has studied at a Muslim madrasa. However, due to political correctness, they are not going to ask such a direct question. Therefore, thousands of young male applicants who are clearly not a threat to anyone have to tediously look up the addresses and telephone numbers of all the places where they have studied when their only crime was being male.

Probably the most ambiguous question (Question 13) is the one which requires that the applicant list all "Professional, Social and Charitable Organizations to Which You Belong (Belonged) or Contribute (Contributed) or with Which You Work (Have Worked)" (DS-157). Can one not see how difficult it is for a man to remember *every* group to which he has *ever* had *any* connection to whatsoever? Obviously, the point of this question is to determine whether the applicant has ever had any ties to any radical group. But again, political correctness forbids such a direct question. As a result, thousands of innocent young men are forced to answer a difficult, tedious, and ambiguous question.

Probably the silliest question (Question 12) is the one that asks the applicants to list the two previous jobs that they have held. Again, it is also required to list the addresses and telephone numbers of these jobs. What is ridiculous about this question is that even terrorists have respectable "day jobs."

One other noteworthy question (Question 15) is the one asking the applicant whether he has ever done military service. Think of how many men could, unfortunately, be able to answer, "Yes, but only because it was sexistly forced onto me."

There is no question that the United States of America needed to do something following the attacks of

September 11 in order to ensure that such an event never occurred again. Indeed, a number of important steps were taken. It is in large part thanks to some of these steps that the United States has not suffered another attack. However, there is no need to be sexist about it. What is visible here is the worse use of political correctness. To have required this form of all Muslim applicants only would have been seen as discrimination. However, requiring it on the basis of sex is—assuming, of course, that it goes against men!—apparently not discrimination. Therefore, all men between the ages of 16 and 45 have been forced to fill out this ridiculous form. This includes men from such allied countries as Poland and the Republic of Georgia, many of whom have served alongside the US military in the War on Terror. This is an incredible insult to such close allies. In the end, "doing something" just to say that something has been done is worse than doing nothing at all. This stupid form does not make the United States of America any safer whatsoever.

It is also important to note that the Russians now require a separate visa application of all US citizens in which all of the above-mentioned questions are included. One cannot blame the Russians for this. Indeed, at least the Russians are not being sexist in their visa application form requirements, as all US citizens are required to fill out the longer form.

What is worse is the potential that this form has to set a nasty precedent. While it may be true that this form—at least on the surface—does not make it more difficult for men to obtain US visas, that is not to say that some other country could not later make it more difficult or even impossible for men of a certain age (or women for that matter) to obtain visas. It is also possible that someday, countries may require visas for men of a certain age, whereas women would be allowed to travel visa-free. While it may be a bit of a stretch to suggest that something like that could ever happen, it was even more ridiculous prior to 2002 (the year in which this form was introduced) to think that there could ever be a case of a country introducing sexist visa application requirements.

What is particularly infuriating about this example is that unlike many of the other examples of sex discrimination against men—such as sexist military conscription laws—this cannot be blamed as simply being a holdover from an old system, as it was enacted in 2002. The existence of this form, therefore, proves that the notion that it is acceptable to discriminate against men is sadly still alive. Indeed, what is even more disturbing is the lack of controversy.

The good news is that the United States is slowly moving away from this form. Increasingly, more and more US consulates around the world are adopting an online-based application—DS-160—one that is designed to replace all previous forms, including this supplemental DS-157 form. Within a few years, it is likely that this form will have thankfully disappeared. This is a good thing for several reasons. First of all, less paperwork is always a good thing.

More importantly, surely, the United States of America does not want to project a sexist, anti-male imagine around the world.

The "Hawk Tuah" Girl

In the past month, a short clip of a young woman saying "hawk tuah" has gone viral. As a men's rights advocate, I was asked by a fellow men's rights advocate to write a short article about my thoughts on this.

The first thing I wanted to mention is the intactivism element. Indeed, I am on a number of intactivist pages on Facebook, and it was on these pages that I first learned about the existence of this video. In fact, I mistakenly thought at first—a tad of wishful thinking, I suppose—that the statement was pro-intactivism.

The reason this clip appeared on intactivism pages is because using spit as a lubricant is usually unnecessary on intact men. Indeed, one of the MANY benefits of the foreskin is that it creates its own natural lubricant. As a result, the glans of an intact man is quite smooth, as it is supposed to be. This shows yet again one of the many disadvantages of circumcision, which is often rightly called "male genital mutilation." For the record, it has ZERO advantages. Since this girl was in the Untied States, sadly, most of the men she has been with were probably cut. Indeed, if they had all been intact, she probably would not have thought such a thought in the first place!

The second thought I had was that it was actually nice for her to show compassion and understanding towards men and their sexual desires. As a men's rights advocate, I have seen a number of striking parallels between feminists and traditionalists. This point brings up two of them. First of all, society has always shown a lack of empathy towards males. In this clip, she shows men empathy. Second, both groups can be quite uptight with sexuality, even though human sexuality is beautiful and should be embraced. We as a society need to be more open with sexuality. It was great to see her so willing to discuss something like this so openly. Side note unrelated to men's rights: I deeply value my Christian faith, and while I feel that Christianity has contributed immensely to civilization and, indeed, is the bedrock of Western Civilization, uptightness with sexuality has been one of its shortcomings.

The third and final thought I had ties into my last point: I have seen a meme floated by those who advocate for traditional society saying "what we think men want (with a picture of her)," juxtaposed with another picture saying "what men actually want (with a picture of a man with a wife and children)." I say men can and should want both. No, that is NOT a reference to adultery, which is absolutely abhorrent! The point is that men can and should want both a wife and family and a vibrant sex life with said wife.

Even though this clip went viral so quickly, I am not sure whether her identity has been revealed, but whoever she is, she seems really amazing!

The Conservative Case in Favor of San Francisco's Proposed Ban on Male Circumcision

San Francisco can be a pretty nutty place. With a ban on Happy Meals, purposely refusing to enforce federal immigration laws, and constantly sending Nancy Pelosi back to Congress, it is easy to see why people would think that anything that comes out of San Francisco must be crazy. However, when this Tea Party Patriot first heard about San Francisco's proposed ban on male circumcision, I found myself saying something I thought I never would: BRAVO SAN FRANCISCO!!!

However, I soon read online comments by some of my fellow Conservatives denigrating this ballot initiative as being more lunacy from San Francisco. I found this quite unfortunate, as the Intactivist movement—like the Men's Movement in general—is actually nonpartisan and has supporters from the Left, the Right, and everything in between. It is for this reason that I decided to write an article to my fellow Conservatives (I actually consider myself to be a Conservative/Libertarian hybrid) in support of San Francisco's ballet initiative and Intactivism in general.

First, let me begin with a brief history of circumcision in the US. I truly believe that if everyone simply knew the history of circumcision in the US, that alone might be enough to bring this barbaric procedure to an end in this otherwise civilized country. Circumcision began in the US and other countries of the Anglosphere during the sexually oppressive Victorian Era towards the end of the 19th century as a way to prevent or "cure" masturbation, which was wrongfully believed to be sinful at the time. Prior to that time, circumcision was quite rare in the US. Unfortunately, by the time that most of society got beyond this absurd fear of masturbation, the practice had sadly become institutionalized. It was at this point that all kinds of myths about it being cleaner and healthier began to set in, myths which sadly continue to the present day.

There is nothing dirty or unhealthy about intact penises, and I, for one, highly resent being called dirty and unhealthy. Quite the contrary, the foreskin plays an important function in the health of the penis. The glans are supposed to remain moist, and the foreskin helps to keep it that way, making the foreskin roughly analogous to the eyelid. It also protects the glans. Likewise, far from being dirty, smegma acts as a natural lubricant and actually contains anti-viral and anti-bacterial properties. Besides, smegma is only occasionally present, and women have smegma as well. Therefore, it is intact penises which are healthier. In the end, if intact penises are dirty, than vaginas must be filthy. I, however, think that both intact penises and vaginas are perfectly clean.

At this point, though, I wish to begin the main point of this article: why Intactivism should be of high appeal to Conservatives.

1) It's American

This point may seem strange at first glance. After all, the majority of American men are circumcised. However, as I just pointed out, circumcision did not begin in the US until the last few decades of the 19th century. That means that the original settlers in places like Jamestown and Plymouth, along with the Founding Fathers, the Revolutionary War veterans, the pioneers moving westward, the Civil War veterans, and the cowboys of the Old West, were almost all intact. I challenge anyone to tell me that these men weren't real Americans. More recently, a number of prominent American men from different walks of life are intact. These include baseball players like Hank Aaron, football players like Joe Namath, and NASCAR drivers such as Richard Petty (source: www.circumstitions.com). What could be more American than baseball, football, and NASCAR? Moreover, there are numerous good Conservative men who are intact, including Ronald Reagan and Marco Rubio (source: www.circumstitions.com). Finally, the American public is increasingly becoming more informed about this, and it is estimated that the circumcision rate amongst newborns in the US has fallen to 33%. As circumstitions.com points out: "The role of infant circumcision in the United States of America is mysterious. The US is the only country in the world where the majority [perhaps it has recently become the minority!] of baby boys have part of their penises cut off for non-religious reasons. Yet this extraordinary custom is very much taken for granted. If it were being introduced today, it would certainly be rejected as barbaric and un-American." http://www.circumstitions.com/USA.html. Therefore, being *intact* is what is actually American.

2) It's Certainly Western

In addition to having a strong sense of national pride, we on the Right are also proud of the Western Civilization heritage of the US. Indeed, while we realize that other civilizations have contributed to humanity as well (and we also realize that the West has had some unsavory moments in history), we are often rightly proud of the many contributions that the United States of America has made to this fabulous civilization. As a citizen of three Western countries—to all three of which I feel a strong sense of national pride—I am especially proud of Western Civilization and the numerous contributions that it has made towards humanity, from the city-states of Ancient Greece to the present day. With the exception of the US and other English-speaking countries since the late 19th century, circumcision has never been practiced within Western Civilization. As for the other Anglosphere countries, they have all either dropped circumcision altogether (such as the UK and New Zealand) or have rates that have now fallen below 20% of male newborns today (such as Australia and Canada). I am therefore confident that the US and the other countries of the Anglosphere will once again be like the rest of civilized Western Civilization, where this barbaric procedure is almost unheard of.

3) It's Christian

Many people mistakenly think that circumcision is a part of the Christian faith. While it is true that circumcision is mentioned in the Old Testament and that Our Lord and Savior Jesus Christ was circumcised, it is not true that it is a part of the Christian faith. After all, many things that are mentioned in the Old Testament, such as the Passover meal and kosher food laws, are also not a part of the Christian faith. Indeed, there are numerous passages in the New Testament that mention that circumcision is not necessary for Christians. There are other New Testament passages that even condemn it. "For whether or not a man is circumcised means nothing; what matters is to obey God's commandments" (I Corinthians 17:19). "Watch out for those who do evil things, those dogs, like cutting the body. It is we, not they, who have received the true circumcision, for we worship God by means of his Spirit and rejoice in our life in union with Christ Jesus. We do not put any trust in external ceremonies" (Philippians 3:2-3). There are numerous other examples of such quotes throughout the New Testament. For Christians, baptism replaced circumcision.

With the notable exception of parts of Africa, the United States is one of the few countries in the world in which Christian men are circumcised. Indeed, to many people in other parts of the world, it is shocking that Christian men in the US are circumcised. In many parts of the world (such as the Balkans, Caucasus, and parts of Asia) where Christianity meets Islam, being intact, along with eating pork and drinking alcohol, is one of the characteristics that distinguishes Christian men from Muslim ones. Here in the Caucasus, the Christian Georgian, Armenian, and Russian men are intact, whereas the Muslim Turks, Azeri, Kurdish, Iranian, Chechen, and Dagestani men are cut. Therefore, most Christian men (except for certain parts of Africa) in other parts of the world are intact. In fact, the Catholic Church actually forbad circumcision in 1442 (source: http://www.historyofcircumcision.net/index.php?option=com_content&task=view&id=28&Itemid=0). Therefore, it is being intact that is a part of the Christian identity. I myself strongly value my Christian faith.

4) It's Pro Individual

We on the Right have always valued the individual and his/her right to make his/her own decisions. Therefore, shouldn't males be allowed to decide for themselves whether they wish to be circumcised? I hasten to emphasize that the proposed ban in San Francisco only applies to those under 18 and, therefore, does not affect adult men who wish to be circumcised. I recently attended an Intactivist rally in Washington where I held a sign which stated the strongest argument we Intactivists have: "his penis, his choice; let your son decide."

5) It's *Not* Government Interference

We on the Right have always rightfully been concerned about government interference in our lives. Indeed, it often upsets us when we see how many other people fail to recognize the dangers of excessive government interference. However, banning male circumcision is not an example of government interference in the lives of private citizens. After all, parents are not allowed to beat their children or to have any other form of cosmetic surgery or body modification (such as tattooing) done to their children. Circumcision is purely elective cosmetic surgery, as the health claims are dubious at best and have to be weighed against stronger health and sexual reasons for leaving the penis intact. Therefore, it is not a big brother government intrusion to ban male circumcision on minors.

6) It's Pro Equality

We on the Right are often accused of being anti-equality, even in favor of discrimination. However, the truth is that we Conservatives are the ones who actually believe in equality. After all, the Left's concept of equality is basically "the absence of discrimination against any group that we feel has historically been oppressed." The Left is, at best, indifferent about reverse discrimination or examples of discrimination against a group that they believe to have always been privileged. By contrast, we on the Right believe that two wrongs don't make a right. As a result, we believe that racial discrimination against White people is just as wrong as racial discrimination against Blacks and other nonwhite people. Likewise, discrimination against men is just as wrong as discrimination against women. The law rightfully forbids *all* forms of genital cutting of girls. This includes a variant in which only the clitoral hood is removed. In fact, the law even forbids a symbolic pinprick of the labia in order to draw one drop of ceremonial blood, regardless of the religious or cultural heritage of the parents. Clearly, male circumcision is more intrusive and more damaging than either of these two above-mentioned examples. For one thing, it certainly isn't any less intrusive or damaging. Therefore, if those two examples of female genital cutting are both illegal, then shouldn't male circumcision also be illegal? If girls are entitled to genital integrity—and they certainly are!—then why are boys, in the spirit of equality, not also entitled to genital integrity?

7) It Leads to Increased Sexual Pleasure

We on the Right are often wrongly thought of as being uptight with human sexuality. While there are certainly uptight prudes on our side, it is we Conservatives who are actually the ones who are more open with sexuality, as the Left has been infected with the anti-sexual views of Feminists. That being said, if we Conservatives are the ones who are pro-sexuality, then we should oppose circumcision since it leads to decreased sexual pleasure in both men and their female partners. Let's not forget that the only reason circumcision began in the US was to prevent or "cure" masturbation, which was wrongfully seen as being sinful at the time. It was, therefore, **designed** to reduce sexual pleasure. While there is no question that circumcised men do indeed enjoy sex, it is clearly not as pleasurable for them as it is for intact men. One man who was circumcised as an adult describes the difference as going from color television to black and white.

Some proponents of circumcision have made the ridiculous argument that American women would reject intact men. This argument is both ridiculous and insulting to American women. Millions of American women are happily married to intact men, both foreign-born and domestic-born. Millions of American women have fallen in love with and ended up dating or even marrying European and Latin American men who are mainly intact. After all, think of all the college coeds who study abroad every year, hoping to date a local guy (who, depending on the country, would almost certainly be intact) while overseas. Likewise, millions of intact men—myself included—have been intimate with at least one American woman in our lifetimes. Many American women, after having experienced an intact man for the first time, find that they prefer it. Indeed, a number of studies of women who have been with both cut and intact men clearly show that women prefer intact penises. This is not surprising, as the gliding motion of the foreskin during sex offers additional pleasure to both the male and his female partner. As a result, many American women who are married to cut men wished that their husbands had been left intact. Therefore, leave your son intact, not just for his pleasure but also for the enjoyment of his future girlfriend/wife.

8) It's Cost Effective

Every year, hundreds of millions of dollars (perhaps even billions) are wasted on circumcisions in the US, much of that at taxpayers' expense through Medicaid. We on the Right are against such a needless waste of money. How outrageous to be wasting such a huge amount of money on brutal cosmetic surgery with health claims that are dubious at best.

9) It's Anti-Junk Science

We on the right are often accused of being anti-science. However, skepticism against junk science is actually what is pro-science. Claims that circumcision reduces the risk of AIDS infection are based on highly flawed studies carried out in Africa by people who were in favor of circumcision before the studies even began. These studies were designed to reach the conclusion that circumcision is beneficial and not to find out whether it is beneficial. Besides, note the obvious piece of evidence against this conclusion: the US has the highest rate of circumcision in the developed world and one of the highest rates of AIDS in the developed world. So much for that hypothesis! In short, this is the same junk science that gave us the hoax of global warming, which we on the Right are now fighting so hard against.

There is so much more to say about this topic, but I have probably gone on too long already. I suggest that all of you log on to some great websites where you will find the truth about circumcision: www.nocirc.org, www.circumstitions.com, www.intactamerica.org, www.cirp.org, www.noharmm.org, and www.doctorsopposingcircumcision.org, amongst other great sites. If only everybody in the US would log on to these sites, this needless, destructive cruelty would come to an immediate end.

To my fellow Conservatives: just because this initiative is from San Fransicko does not automatically mean that it is an example of left-wing lunacy. After all, a broken clock is right twice a day. Besides, this effort was initiated by the good people of San Fransicko, unlike the ban on Happy Meals which was passed by their nutty city council. Intactivism is actually nonpartisan and, as I have pointed out, is what is most logical from a Conservative point of view. Since Intactivism is nonpartisan, perhaps a fellow Intactivist who is left-leaning should write a companion article to this one.

To San Franciscans: the next time you go out and do something crazy like banning Happy Meals—and I'm sure you will (I actually say that affectionately in this context)—realize that I will always have a soft spot in my heart for you after this. I promise to try to erase "San Fransicko" from my vocabulary. I will also state for the record that I had the pleasure of visiting your beautiful city back in 2003, and I enjoyed it.

To Rush Limbaugh personally: whenever I am in the US, I often listen to your radio show. Indeed, I first started listening to you at the age of 14 back in 1991. While I usually agree with what you say, you have, on occasion, made fun of the fabulous Intactivist group NOCIRC. I find this unfortunate. I have spoken with the leadership of NOCIRC, and they have told me that they would love to talk to you. I know for myself personally it would be a huge honor to talk to you.

I am myself proud to be an intact Conservative/Libertarian Republican Christian American/Western happily married man. There is absolutely nothing contradictory about any of that. In fact, *that* is what is actually most logical.

Special Occasions

Nearly every culture has special occasions. This is to be expected. After all, in our lives, regardless of our religious/national/ethnic/cultural backgrounds, there are major events that distinguish certain days as being far more significant than "yet another ordinary day." Unsurprisingly, many of these special occasions the world over mark the same life events. This is because we all experience many of the same life events. As a personal side note, as a world traveler (I have up to 120 countries on 6 continents visited at the time of writing), there are two things that strike me the most in all of my travels: a) how different we all are culturally, and at the same time: b) just how similar we all really are at the end of the day.

The two most notable life events are the first and last: birth and death. Obviously, we all experience these two events the world over, regardless of our backgrounds. Naturally, there are ceremonies connected to these two events, such as baptisms and funerals (see the article I wrote about Georgian funerals, which appears earlier in this half of this book).

Besides the obvious examples of birth and death, two other notable life events are finishing education and getting married, which come with ceremonies such as graduations and weddings. It is at this point that I wish to remark on how the concept of marriage has existed throughout history in nearly every culture of the world. Granted, the concept is not always the same, i.e., whether marriage is monogamous or polygamous and the extent to which it is intended to be a lifetime commitment. However, the fact that its existence is near universal is an indication that it is a fabulous concept and that society absolutely needs to re-embrace it.

One of the many reasons I got involved with the men's rights movement is because I was horrified by how anti-marriage many feminists are, and I wanted to fight to save marriage. It is for this reason that I was heartbroken that many men have gone MGTOW. As a side note to those of you who are MGTOW, while I have made some somewhat harsh comments about you in the past, I have come to fully understand why, based on the present situation, you have chosen this path. As a men's rights advocate, I am fighting to fix the reasons that led you to go MGTOW.

I plan to address the issue of gender equality and weddings later in this article. However, at this point, I wish to first discuss coming-of-age celebrations. Many non-Western—especially more traditional—societies have an elaborate coming-of-age celebration. This is not surprising, considering that passing from childhood into adulthood is one of the biggest stages of life.

Depending on the country/culture, coming of age may or may not involve some sort of an initiation (Remember, this proposed CEDAM treaty calls for an end to all pain rite of passage ceremonies for both boys and girls, especially if they involve permanently marking the body, most especially if they involve genital cutting.)

Western societies, by contrast, really don't have coming-of-age ceremonies. In the case of the United States, other than some Native American tribes, there are basically only two communities that have coming-of-age ceremonies: the Jewish community and the Hispanic community. These two examples are perfect for illustrating the sexist double standards vis-à-vis males with regards to coming-of-age ceremonies specifically and overall societal attitudes in general.

In both cases, each ceremony was for one sex only: in the case of the Jewish community, the Bar Mitzvah was for boys only, and in the case of the Hispanic community, the quinciera was for girls only. There was indeed a logical reason for this in both cases. In the Jewish case, in order for a Jewish service to be legitimate, there have to be at least ten adult Jewish men present. Once a 13-year-old boy has had his bar mitzvah, he is considered an adult Jewish man in this context. Granted, Jewish girls came of age, too, but it did not have the same significance. Therefore, this tradition was for boys only.

In the Hispanic community, the quinciera was for girls only. Again, there was a logic to that as well. The thinking was that when a girl turned 15, she was ready for marriage. This was the family's way of presenting her to potential suitors. Granted, young boys aren't out courting girls. Still, the notion of boys coming onto the dating scene was not the same. Therefore, this tradition was for girls only.

Understandably, the Jewish girls felt left out. As a result, the Bat Mitzvah was created for them. However, there still is no equivalent for Hispanic boys, no "quinciero." Why do I have a sneaking suspicion that if it were the other way around, i.e., only Jewish girls and only Hispanic boys had a coming-of-age tradition, the Hispanic girls would have long fought for and gotten their equivalent, and the Jewish boys would still have nothing?!

The irony in this is that, if anything, the Jewish tradition still holds at least some of its original meaning. By contrast, even in the most traditional countries of Latin America, nobody thinks of 15-year-old girls as ready for marriage anymore. And yet, the Jewish one is the one that ended up with an opposite-sex equivalent. Nothing better illustrates society's indifference to males regarding special moments than this contrast.

It is at this point that I wish to discuss sexism and weddings. Obviously, wedding traditions vary considerably from religion to religion, culture to culture, country to country, and even generation to generation. Here, I wish to discuss the ones which are unfair to men. Indeed, there are even some people who think that weddings should be mainly or even exclusively about the bride. Clearly, weddings should be equally about the bride and the groom. As a result, both families should contribute equally to both the wedding and the honeymoon.

Another point about weddings is the bride walking down the aisle. A better tradition would be for the bride and the groom to walk down the aisle together, as that places an equal emphasis on both. I am happy to say my wife and I did this at our wedding.

This example perfectly illustrates why those of us who fight for women's rights and those of us who fight for men's rights ought to be partners rather than adversaries. After all, when I have mentioned this to some feminists, they say that they like this better, as they don't like the symbolism of the bride being handed off from one man to another. As a men's rights advocate, I like this better because I don't think the bride should get all of the attention, whereas the groom gets zero.

One final note about weddings: it warms my heart to see the growth in male engagement rings. It's great to see more women take the initiative to propose marriage to their boyfriends.

The final examples of special occasions that I wish to address in this article are International Women's Day and International Men's Day. First of all, there is the obvious issue: that International Women's Day is far more commonly recognized than International Men's Day. Worse yet, as I mentioned in Article 1, in the former Soviet Union, there was a Veterans Day (This is still the case in Russia), which was seen unofficially as a male equivalent to International Women's Day. Indeed, it greatly upsets me when people point this out to me, knowing that I am a men's rights advocate, thinking that I would be happy to hear this, i.e., that Russia has a men's day. In reality, it perfectly illustrates the very mindset I am fighting against: that men only get acknowledged with regards to doing military service, which was sexistly forced upon them, whereas women get a special day for merely existing. This combination is the worst-case scenario. Having only a women's day with no men's day is better than this arrangement.

From now on, let's make sure that special occasions include men just as much as they include women.

The Crux of the Issue

As I have mentioned in one of my recent articles for the National Coalition For Men (NCFM), I have been a member of NCFM for a little over a decade now, and I have been active in fighting for gender equality for males since at least January of 1989, a month before I turned 12. In the course of all of these years, I have had many discussions—often angry and heated!—with regards to the numerous issues which uniquely or disproportionately affect males. The more I think about it, the more I have come to realize the exact problem with most of the situation: our different views of the past.

I remember that someone once asked Cassie Jaye why feminists and men's rights advocates cannot work together since we both claim to fight for gender equality. She totally nailed the answer: the problem is patriarchy theory.

Feminists hold that in the past and into the present, society was and still is governed by a patriarchy that privileges men and oppresses women. As a result of this system, it is simply physically impossible for sexism against men to exist. Some feminists would occasionally give us the "patriarchy harms men too" line, though even that has become rare. Likewise, some feminists—sometimes the same ones—would also occasionally admit that feminism may have gone too far, though that line is also not frequently heard these days either.

Therefore, to those who believe this, bringing up men's issues makes them defensive, as there simply cannot be any legitimate issues to bring up, as the existence of said issues is physically impossible. Therefore, those of us who are fighting for men's rights are, at best, being silly. At worst, it is a ruse to take away women's rights.

As a men's rights advocate, I reject the notion of patriarchy theory. Like a lot of false beliefs, it starts out with pieces of reality here and there, which are stitched together—all the while ignoring examples that go the other way—to create a template. This newly created template is then blown out of proportion, and all of reality is forced to match the template. Finally, the template is then applied to every aspect of life, even in completely unrelated matters. The concept becomes repeated enough times that it becomes a reality, and woe unto anyone who dares to disagree with it, especially if (in this particular case) you are a man.

But is it true? Well, on the surface of it, one can certainly see evidence that points in that direction. After all, the vast majority of society's leaders throughout history have been men, and this is true in nearly every society on the planet, regardless of factors such as religion, race/ethnicity, location, level of development, etc. Likewise, nearly all occupations were mostly male. Furthermore, the husband/father was said to be the head of the household.

However, as is often the case, the reality was far more nuanced and not nearly so one-sided. First of all, in terms of those with leadership positions, while they were mostly men, most men would go their whole lives without ever having so much as a conversation with a man with a position of authority, let alone actually being a man with a position of authority himself. Was the male peasant farmer truly privileged over the female peasant farmer because the king was himself a man?

Likewise, patriarchy theory totally ignores the things that go the other way, such as chivalry and male disposability, especially with regards to military service obligations. Indeed, traditional society was not patriarchal; it was chivalrous, and chivalry is literally "ladies first." This was especially noteworthy in life-threatening situations such as getting off of sinking ships. Patriarchy theory holds that men have all the power and that they use it to oppress women. However, when in world history has a group of oppressors ever valued the lives of the people they were oppressing over their own?

Instead, the thinking was that men and women each had different but complementary roles to play. Up until a few generations ago, most jobs involved heavy lifting. Men, with their stronger upper body strength, were better suited for such jobs. Even more importantly, since it is women who get pregnant, give birth, and breastfeed, it is women who stay home to raise the children. Put the two together, and society created a system where men build, run, maintain, and defend society, whereas women would raise the next generation to do the same. Basically, the old system (I refuse to call it a "patriarchy"), for all its faults—and there were many!—was at least based on mutual love and respect.

You may be saying that at this point, well, that may have been the intention, but men still got the better deal. First of all, I would point you to the essay that appeared earlier about "My Modest Proposal." Second of all, there have been millions of women who have now had the chance to try it both ways, i.e., have a career on the one hand and stay at home with children on the other. So many have said they preferred the latter. It's almost as if the old system was set up that way because that is what women prefer!

I say this not to encourage a return to the past. If I were in favor of a return to traditional gender roles, I would merely be a traditionalist and not a men's rights advocate. If anything, I don't think that would be fair to men! In fact, many of us in the men's rights movement like to joke that those of you who think that men's rights advocates wish to return to the past don't know the first thing about us: many of us feel that the past was at least as unfair to men as it was to women. That being said, most of us would emphasize that this is not a competition to see who had it worse, and such discussions lead us in the wrong direction. Likewise, many of the traditional gender roles we had—including some of those that I fight against as a men's rights advocate—were a necessity of the time.

Instead, my goal here is to show that the old system did not merely privilege men and that there were advantages to being a woman. The way forward is to set up society in a way that both men and women have the opportunity to experience both having a career and staying home with children within the confines of marriage and the nuclear family. And best of all, no one is ever drafted!

One final note about "the crux of the issue": the surprising amount of overlap between traditionalists and feminists. At first glance, it would appear as if the two groups could not be more different. Indeed, there are some red-button issues where the two groups are on exact opposite sides. Furthermore, the two groups loathe each other. However, the old saying that politics makes odd bedfellows comes into play here. The main reason is that both groups are gynocentric. I am assuming that I need not explain how feminists are gynocentric. However, traditionalists are also gynocentric in that they are chivalrous, and chivalry is literally "ladies first." Also, both groups are uptight with sexuality. Indeed, they are often on the same side with regards to issues such as pornography and prostitution. I call this unlikely coalition between traditionalists and feminists "the gynocentric alliance." Along with the alliance between Western leftists and Islamists, it is probably the most unholy alliance in the entire political/social history of Western Civilization. One other example of an unholy alliance within Europe is nationalists on the right together with Marxists on the left, opposing European Union membership.

It is a bit of an oversimplification but still a fair generalization to say that the political right is dominated by traditionalists, who are gynocentric, and the political left is dominated by feminists, who are gynocentric. As a result of this situation, neither side is a natural ally for the men's rights movement, in spite of the fact that we are fighting for the *actual* gender equality that the vast majority of society claims to want.

Generally speaking, these unholy alliances are usually on the wrong side. The above-mentioned examples are no exception. We should have actual gender equality. Likewise, human sexuality—along with openness with it— is a beautiful thing that we should embrace, in spite of the unfortunate uptightness that both traditionalists and feminists have shown it.

How Men's Rights Has Made Me Anti-War

One completely unexpected effect that being in the men's rights movement has had on me is that it has made me very anti-war. Granted, I have always been staunchly anti-draft. However, I used to be more open to the idea of using force to overthrow brutal dictators. After all, you have to talk to bullies in the only language that they understand. While I still think that there is some validity to that argument, I have come to see how that can cause more problems than it solves.

The main point here, however, is less about the present day and more about history in general. I have come to see the way that men, especially young men, and even boys, have been used as cannon fodder throughout history, often against their will. Worse yet, they were often drafted to fight against what their natural interests would be. For example, the Ottoman Turks often drafted young Christian boys to fight for the Ottoman Empire. Obviously, their natural interest would be to see their lands freed from Ottoman rule. While they were usually sent to fight in parts of the empire away from their own homelands, they were still forced to fight for the entity that was occupying their homelands. Another example of this phenomenon is that rebel groups moving through a village often draft many young men into their ranks, whether they agree with the rebels' cause or not.

The main flaw with war is that it seems to be predicated on the notion that the winning side was the more virtuous one. However, we can all see examples throughout history of where that was not the case. It is at this point that I would also wish to dispel the notion that many on the political left have that the losing side was the losing side because they were a more peaceful people, and the winning side was the winning side because they were more aggressive. It is worth noting that so many of the world's nations/ethnic groups, etc., have been both the conquerors and the conquered at some point in their histories. Therefore, in the majority of wars, there were no "good guys" or "bad guys"; there were just simply two different groups of people (often two different nations) that simply wanted as much territory as possible.

Another problem with war is just how wasteful it is. Beyond the obvious cost in terms of the lives lost on the battlefield and civilian casualties, there is also the cost of national treasure. War requires that much money be spent on military equipment, salaries of the soldiers, supply lines of food and medical supplies, etc. Was there seriously no better way for different countries (or other entities) to resolve their disputes than to send the strongest, healthiest young men they had to kill each other in Roman-style gladiator games that took place in a field rather than an arena?!

It is at this point that I wish to address what has been the biggest failure of the Christian faith: its failure to prevent war. I deeply value my Christian faith, and Christianity has probably made more positive contributions to humanity than anything else in world history. Nonetheless, it is shocking that church leaders so failed to prevent war between fellow Christians. I have often wondered why no pope took it upon himself to stop the war between at least fellow Catholics if not Christians in general. He should have written a charter and gotten all Catholic kings to sign it, which would have banned war between fellow Catholics. This charter should have created a tribunal where all disputes, such as territory between rival kingdoms or disagreements as to who the rightful heir to the throne is, could be brought and resolved fairly and peacefully. Obviously, I am not naïve as to not realize that such a tribunal would have been prone to corruption. However, it certainly would have been a far better system. The thought of fellow Christians killing each other in battle when the two groups of men were otherwise quite similar to each other—it was just that they came from different countries and spoke different languages (In some cases, even that was not true)—is indeed heartbreaking.

It is at this point that I wish to give two particularly noteworthy examples of pointless wars that should have been prevented. The first one is the War of the Roses. The House of York and the House of Lancaster both made claims to the throne of England since there was no obvious heir. It was a brutal civil war in which thousands died, often peasant farmers who were pulled off of their fields while knowing little about the issue they were fighting over. There had to have been a better way to determine which family had a stronger claim to the throne of England.

Another example is the war of the Spanish Succession. A little background: in the early 18th century, King Charles II of Spain (or Carlos II in Spanish) was so heavily inbred (even more so than royal standards in general) that he could not have children. Foreseeing an opening on the Spanish throne, French king Louis XIV suggested that his grandson could become the king of Spain, as Louis was married to Charles's sister. However, he was also in line to become the king of France. If he were allowed to become the king of Spain, then someday he would be in a position to merge the two large, powerful Catholic countries (both of which had large empires in the Americas at the time) of France and Spain together. Needless to say, many of the other European countries, such as Austria, Britain, and Portugal, did not want to see that happen.

This resulted in a war. The war ended with the Treaty of Utrecht. Under the terms, Louis's grandson was permitted to become the king of Spain, but the king of France and the king of Spain could never be the same person. I remember studying this in my European history class in high school thinking it took an entire war with how many thousands dead on both sides to simply reach that conclusion!

This brings me to the issue of the draft. It is shocking that so many people support what is tantamount to a form of slavery. After all, the two-word definition of slavery is "involuntary servitude." Again, I am not naïve. I realize that throughout most of world history, if a society didn't have a draft, it could have been overrun by another one that did have a draft. After this, the invading side could have moved in and imposed their will on the people they conquered by forcing them to convert to their religion, adopt names from their language, and force them to speak their language. Worse yet, they could have turned them into slaves. On top of all of that, they then could have drafted the conquered people into *their* army. If there is one thing I can agree with the pro-conscription crowd, it is indeed better to be drafted into your own army rather than a foreign one! And by the way, all of the above is assuming that the invading army didn't simply massacre the entire conquered nation!

Often when I speak out against conscription, people point to defeating the Nazis in World War II. However, they are only looking at the issue on the surface. The Nazis came to power following the disaster that was World War I. Indeed, while I gave two examples above of wars that were particularly stupid and destructive, World War I was probably the stupidest and most destructive war in all of world history. The worst part is the fact that as destructive as that war was, the real destruction would come later, as it was out of the ashes of this war that the Nazis came to power in Germany, and the communists came to power in Russia. Obviously, from these two disasters came World War II, the Holocaust, the Cold War, Soviet oppression of central

Europe, and so many other horrible things. If only World War I had been prevented.

This is where anti-conscription comes into play. If there hadn't been a draft for World War I, either the war would have never happened, or it would have been over much quicker with far less destruction, and probably would not have led to either Nazi Germany or communist Russia. Indeed, while I realize that there would have been no way to have enforced this if there had never been any draft—coupled with not shaming men into fighting—ever, throughout the whole of world history, there would have been far fewer wars. It is centuries past the time that the world should have moved beyond using young men as disposable cannon fodder against their will. Instead, countries need to realize that these men represent their futures. These men should instead be building things.

Sadly, in many countries, a running peacetime draft became the norm for generations, a coming-of-age rite of passage. It has also been a long time since society moved away from this. Instead, there has been some talk of creating a culture of voluntary national service, in which the majority of young people, both male and female, upon coming of age, would do a form of voluntary national service, of which military service would be an option. What I like about this idea is that it would be voluntary, not sexist, and would not have to involve military service. I myself served in the Peace Corps after graduating from college. For the record, I am not trying to imply that Peace Corps service is the same thing as military service. Instead, the point is that we all have different talents and different ways to serve our countries better.

One final note about defense and anti-war/anti-conscription: the European Union (yes, I realize that it was not called that back then) nearly ended up with a united military back in the 1950s. Sadly, the plan failed when the French parliament rejected it. Perhaps the time has come for this plan to be reconsidered. A single military—with zero draft, of course!—to defend the whole of the 27 countries of the European Union would be a great way to ensure peace in Europe, especially if it would already include the candidate countries along with NATO members Norway, Iceland, and hopefully even Britain. Likewise, it would be quite cost-effective as well. As a proud citizen of the European Union myself, I would dearly love to see that happen.

In Defense of "Incels"

I wanted to write this essay in defense of what has to be the most unfairly maligned group in society, the so-called "incels." "Incel" is short for "involuntary celibate." It is a reference to people who want to be sexually active and/or in an intimate partner relationship but are unable to find anyone willing to be with them in such a capacity. It was actually coined by a lesbian in the late 90s to describe her situation. It has since become an insult that feminists are quick to use.

Oftentimes when people disagree with feminists, feminists will frequently claim that that person is merely an incel. When asked to describe an incel, what follows is a description of a violent, abusive jerk. Indeed, the word "incel" often comes with the adjective "violent" in front of it. However, as is often the case, reality cannot be further from the image.

The "jerk appeal" in many women is quite well known. Many women insist on dating abusive loser jerks because they are "oh so much more fun," while the nice guys get ignored or relegated to the friend zone. Indeed, I have heard women remark that some of the nicest guys you will ever meet are the ones without girlfriends. Therefore, the description provided of incels is actually a description of the loser jerks many women insisted on dating, who are, therefore, not incels. The actual incels are usually the polar opposite of the description provided. In fact, far from being arrogant or violent, they are actually much more likely to be self-deprecating.

Even before feminists started using this label as an insult with the totally inaccurate description that they added to it, being an actual incel was indeed a lonely existence. Here they were, everything that society in general and women, in particular, said they were supposed to be (usually without even trying, largely based on their own natural personality), and they had little to no success on the dating scene. By contrast, the guys who did everything wrong typically had no trouble finding women. While in this situation, it seemed as if few even noticed their situation, and fewer still would even care.

As if this weren't bad enough, feminists have made it even harder for them to find dates, as they have turned the whole dating scene into one big minefield through vague, unreasonable sexual harassment rules/metoo, a minefield where the mines can retroactively go off decades after the fact.

Worse yet, feminists also want to take away prostitution/strip clubs, the only way many actual incels (I am using the adjective "actual" to make a contrast between guys who are actually incels versus the 100% inaccurate feminist description of them) can get any sexual fulfillment. Feminists claim that men who go to prostitutes are violent and abusive, when in reality, they are much more likely to be nice, lonely guys who cannot find a woman. I remember reading an article written by a sex worker from Australia (where it is legal) who stated that many of her clients were actually some of the nicest guys you will ever meet. One even spent hours putting together a romantic playlist for his evening with her. Her point was, if you want to know where all the good men have gone, meet the men who come to me!

As if the above-mentioned situation weren't horrible enough, feminists now act like said incels are the most dangerous threat to society. Anytime anyone tries to mention any men's issues, even those which are unrelated to dating and sexuality, feminists will call that person an incel and act like that makes him a horrible thing. This is after many of them encouraged men to speak up about their issues, swearing up and down that they were going to be understanding while actually being vicious. They then wonder why men won't speak up more often. Besides, how does struggling in the dating scene invalidate one's point of view with regards to issues such as sexist military service obligations or boys falling behind academically? Is the amount of sex one has a source of status that lends authority to perspectives on social issues? When it comes to difficulties with regards to the dating scene, shouldn't the ones who are struggling be the ones we listen to the most?

After all of this, many women, upon reaching roughly age 30, complain, "Where have all the good men gone?" It is shocking how they fail to realize that they rejected all the good men when they were in their 20s and could easily have had their pick of them. At this point, doesn't that make them the "incels"? At the same time, they demand and often get empathy for their situation, while men get none when they are in that situation in their 20s. This brings up one of the biggest overall issues with regards to men's rights: the lack of empathy society has always shown males.

This also brings up another issue that is common to men's rights in general but is particularly poignant in this instance: women not knowing what it is like to be a man. I have seen several videos where women, either as an experiment or to help a male friend, set up a dating profile on a dating app. They are quickly shocked to learn just how difficult it is for men. In one very recent video, it was a mere three days after she had set up the profile, and she was devasted to learn just how difficult it was. She even said she was starting to hate women as a result of her experience.

Keep in mind, if people who are themselves women and therefore have a far better idea of how to appeal to women find it extremely difficult, what hope is there for a kind and perhaps socially awkward young man? Furthermore, the women who were doing these experiments probably weren't even thinking about a possible sexual harassment allegation. If only every woman had had this experience at the start of her youth, there would be a lot more empathy, and no one would use the term incel in such a manner.

If ever feminism committed a low blown—and it has committed many!—it did so with the label "incel." If ever there were a group of people who have been unfairly maligned and suffer from a huge lack of empathy, it is young men who are struggling with regards to dating. To those of you in this situation, I know that it may seem as if nobody notices what you are going through. And while it is true that your situation does not get nearly enough attention, there are people like me who do notice you and what you are going through and are advocating on your behalf. I am here for you!

Bavarian Business Attire

Every year during the warmer months of the year, it seems that the perennial debate about where the office air conditioning should be set comes up. Many women complain that the air conditioning is set too low and that, consequently, the offices are too cold. Some even complain that that is sexism. Well, in a sense, they may actually be right, but not for the reasons that they are thinking.

Instead, the real issue is that society requires men to wear long pants and even suits in business settings in warmer weather, whereas women are allowed to wear skirts that go above the knee or lightweight summer dresses. If women can wear skirts that go above the knee, why can't men wear a nice pair of dress shorts?!

I am therefore proposing a new look for liberated men in business settings. I call it "Bavarian Business," as it resembles the traditional folk costume of Bavaria, Germany. The thinking is that in warmer weather, this should be seen as just as dressy and, therefore, just as acceptable as a full business suit would be, regardless of the situation. As to how warm the warmer weather needs to be before a man wears Bavarian Business, it is up to each man to decide for himself. I also wish to emphasize that this is intended to be equivalent to business suits and not tuxedos. Therefore, if the occasion calls for either a black tie or white tie, Bavarian Business would not be acceptable.

The first aspect of Bavarian Business is to substitute long pants for shorts. However, not just any shorts will do. The shorts should be dress shorts, i.e., of the same material as the long pants, but only shorter. The most likely colors would be khaki or navy blue. Cargo shorts and jeans shorts would not be acceptable. The same button dress shirt should be worn, only it would probably be short-sleeved. Other than that, the same dress shoes, socks, and ties should be worn.

I have also added an optional fedora hat to the look. This brings up another sexist issue: why can't men wear hats inside? Some have tried to explain this by claiming that traditionally, women's hats were a part of their outfits, and therefore, they should not have been expected to remove them. However, this explanation does not make sense for several reasons. First of all, the suit hats that men would wear were usually matching their suits and were just as much a part of a man's outfit. Besides, even if it were not a part of his outfit, is that any reason to ask him to remove it? Moreover, if he is wearing it, it is a part of his outfit!

Another explanation is that in the New Testament, Paul instructs women to cover their heads, whereas men are not supposed to cover their heads before God. This explanation makes more sense. However, if this is the reason, then it should apply only to churches and religious settings. I also hasten to point out that most churches no longer require women to cover their heads, whereas men still cannot wear hats. As always, the traditional gender role for women was abolished, whereas the traditional gender role for men lives on.

At this point, I wish to give a shoutout to the women of Iran who are fighting to not have to wear headscarves in public. Worldwide, let's make wearing headcover optional for both men and women in basically all situations.

To those of you who think this would look funny, I am sure we would get used to the look very quickly. Switching to this would benefit both men and women in warmer weather. Also, I hasten to add that I have seen police uniforms in Washington DC and mailman uniforms with shorts. Likewise, wearing shorts in formal settings is common in Bermuda, though the shorts there are a bit too long, and they come with socks that are also too long. Moreover, while it is one thing to consider khaki pants to be dressier than khaki shorts, it is ridiculous to consider jeans to be dressier than khaki shorts.

Some have thought it sexist that women can choose between pants or a skirt, whereas men can only wear pants. Indeed, it is true that there are/have been societies where men can wear skirts, such as some South Pacific cultures. Likewise, there is a skirt that men wrap around themselves in Myanmar. More famously, Scotland has kilts. I myself have a kilt from Scotland and a wrap from Myanmar. Also, in Antiquity, men often wore robes, as did priests. It is worth noting that the French word for "dress" is "robe." There are also graduation gowns worn by both men and women. It is, therefore, not strange for men to wear garments related to skirts or even dresses.

I myself don't have a strong opinion one way or the other as to whether men should be allowed to wear skirts. If we were to allow for that, no doubt more manly skirts would be developed, just as more feminine pants were developed. I am much more interested in men being allowed to wear shorts.

Let's embrace shorts in warmer weather for men so as to free men! As to whether women should also be allowed to wear shorts in business settings in warmer weather, absolutely!

I made a short video on my Youtube channel about this. Here is the link:

https://www.youtube.com/watch?v=p3LeICNRTmk

I Used to Adore Feminism

At first glance, many of you may be shocked by that statement, but it is absolutely true. Indeed, many men's rights advocates are actually former feminists. I have joked that the men's rights movement should be called "the Who's Who of former feminists." First some background.

I first got my start in the men's rights movement when, a month before I turned 12 in January of 1989, I took legal action—without the help or even knowledge of my parents!—against my school on the grounds of sexism against boys. By writing one letter, I singlehandedly caused a federal investigation into my school. For the record, the investigation proved that I was right.

It was at this time that I thought that feminism was so the way to go. I believed the mantra that, in spite of the movement's name, feminism was actually about gender equality in general and that feminism had men covered, too. Furthermore, while I have always valued the Christian faith, I have also always believed that society is too uptight with sexuality. I thought that feminism was open with sexuality. In short, feminism would address the one aspect of traditional Western Civilization that I did not like, namely traditional gender roles along with uptightness with sexuality.

However, it wouldn't take long for me to realize that nothing could be further from the truth. I was soon made aware of the many horrendous misandrist feminist quotes.

Worse yet, any time I would point these quotes to feminists I knew personally, I thought they would immediately disown them, saying something to the effect of "Of course, those are horrible quotes, and such people are an embarrassment to the movement." Instead, these feminists would make excuses for these quotes and never disown them, no matter how horrible they were. The fact that feminists would defend these quotes no matter what was actually far more upsetting than the quotes themselves. I thought about including a list of said quotes in this book, but I ultimately decided against it. I am guessing that most of you are already familiar with many of these quotes.

In addition to the horrible quotes, I soon saw how feminists would deny that sexism against men even exists, even when I would give blatant examples such as sexist military service obligations and higher retirement ages for men. In some cases, they would even try to claim that these are actually examples of sexism against women. Denying that sexism against men even exists when it clearly does is actually the ultimate sexism.

Moreover, like I said, I have always believed in openness with sexuality. I was shocked to find that feminists were often just as uptight with sexuality as traditionalists. It was for these reasons that I would soon no longer support feminism.

However, at this point, I am ready to be proven wrong. If feminists would be willing to work together with men's rights advocates to bring about *actual* gender equality, that would be fabulous.

Final Thoughts

As I made clear in the introduction, I launched this initiative not merely to have a treaty on men's rights just to have one but because such a treaty is clearly needed. I mentioned 46 different examples of outright discrimination or merely issues in which men are uniquely or disproportionally affected. Furthermore, the point of this initiative is not to counteract the fabulous global treaty on women's rights but to complement it. After all, if you wish to free women from traditional gender roles, then you also need to free men from traditional gender roles. Doing so would make the final nail in the coffin for traditional gender roles.

Recently, the Norwegian government had a Men's Equality Commission. The final report was absolutely heartwarming. I wish to quote the great article that Richard Reeve wrote on this commission:

> First, there is a clear rejection of zero-sum thinking. Working on behalf of boys and men does not *dilute* the ideals of gender equality, it *applies* them. Here is how the Commission sets out its stall:
>
> Many boys and men do not feel that equality is about them or exists for them. The men's committee believes that equality's next step should be to include boys and men's challenges to a greater

extent than today... Greater attention to boys' and men's equality challenges will strengthen equality policy, not weaken it. (https://ofboysandmen.substack.com/p/look-to-norway)

The Norwegians also referenced the alarming levels of polarization that gender discussions have reached. The source of said polarization is the zero-sum mindset.

While my first involvement with men's rights came at the age of 11, my real involvement in the movement began when I joined the National Coalition For Men (NCFM) in June of 2010. I am NCFM's (www.ncfm.org) liaison contact for the Republic of Georgia, the international coordinator, and a board member. (For the record, I should state that some of the opinions stated in the essays that appear in this book are not necessarily those of NCFM). Prior to officially joining the movement in 2010, I had long considered it. However, at the same time, I felt something pulling me back, asking me, "Do you really want to get involved with that?" It wouldn't take long for me to see why I was reluctant. I was shocked by the amount of hate I got from people whom I thought were friends and knew me well. Indeed, I have lost friends over this. That being said, I have zero regrets about getting involved. This movement is clearly needed.

It is shocking how quickly some people become so defensive the minute men's issues are mentioned. They immediately start to disagree with everything that is being said without actually listening to what is being said. There have been times when, in such discussions, I would mention my support of issues that went the other way, partly to try and find common ground. Much to my surprise, the other person was still disagreeing with me. In hindsight, I now realize that the other person was in a defensive reflex mode to automatically disagree with whatever I was saying. Please, everyone, stop getting so defensive when men's rights are mentioned. Look at what is actually being proposed here. I hope that if you actually believe in equality, you will agree with most of this proposed treaty. Likewise, you will also see that men's rights, in general, and this proposed treaty specifically, are not a threat to women's rights. On the contrary, it strengthens it.

Like the Norwegians, I, too, have become shocked by the growing levels of polarization. It breaks my heart to see men go MGTOW. One of the many reasons why I got involved with men's rights was because I wanted to save marriage and the family. That being said, I understand why so many of you have gone MGTOW, and I am working to fix those conditions. This proposed global treaty would go a long way in that regard.

Even more alarming is the growing number of people—including women—who now think that it was a mistake to give women the right to vote. I wish to reassure you that nobody in the men's rights movement thinks that. It is incredibly gut-wrenching that society has reached a point of such polarization that people would even suggest such a thing. Can we all please just take a step back from the edge?!

I am currently looking for a country to sponsor this initiative, and I am both willing and indeed eager to work with absolutely anyone who is willing to work with me. I realize that the final version of any treaty may not look like the one I am suggesting. However, I do ask that two issues in particular be avoided: abortion and homosexuality. Those two issues are so polarizing that they could divide people who would otherwise support most of what is in this proposed treaty. That being said, if there is an example of discrimination against women that was not included in CEDAW, such a point could be included in the final version of CEDAM.

My own personal biases, such as my Christian faith, my strong patriotism to all three of the countries in which I hold citizenship, my undying love of the European Union, and my support for such classic liberal ideas such as free market economics and the minimalist state probably became evident in some of the essays included in the second half of this book.

However, the beauty of men's rights—and, by extension, gender equality in general—is that it's for everyone. Indeed, I have seen it remarked that the men's rights movement, without even trying, is a surprisingly diverse group of people. While we are mainly in Western countries, we have members and supporters in a number of non-Western countries, with India being a notable example.

We also have people from across the political spectrum, of all racial and ethnic backgrounds, of different socio-economic backgrounds, and people from all religions and no religion at all. I also wish to strongly emphasize that we have a number of women in our movement. Even within men's rights, different advocates will often emphasize different issues. After all, this initiative mentions 46 different issues.

Together, let's bring an end to this horrible, destructive, and totally pointless gender war. If we could just pass and implement this proposed global treaty, we would all be amazed at how much better the world would be for everyone. We will be wondering what took us so long to address men's issues and why we were ever so reluctant to address them.

I would like to recommend a book and a film, both by former feminists. *The Red Pill* by Cassie Jaye is an amazing movie. Likewise, Norah Vincent tried living as a man for 18 months and was shocked about how difficult it was. I was particularly touched when a reporter asked her if we know what it is like to be men, and she said, "We don't have a clue." Her book is *Self-Made Man.*

I wish to leave you with the three quotes I mentioned at the end of the introduction. The third one mentions three points, and yet these three points cover over half of what is in this proposed treaty. Most of the rest could be covered with the simple notions of equal protection under the law, and love and empathy towards males.

"The biggest example of sexism in the world today is the ridiculous notion that only one sex has ever been the victim of it";

"The unofficial definition of gender equality must never be allowed to be 'the absence of discrimination against women'";

"With nastiness towards none, genital integrity for all, and military service obligations for none, I am a men's rights advocate."

www.ingramcontent.com/pod-product-compliance
Lightning Source LLC
LaVergne TN
LVHW051038070526
838201LV00066B/4849